W9-BEV-036
PROPERTY OF HILLEL ACADEMY

SHE'S HOME ALONE...

The kitchen door opened. "Get out," she said as she shoved the dog out.

Beautiful. He watched her step back into the house and close the door. What luck. What incredible luck. Yeah. Kidnapping was all about mistakes. Mistakes like letting the dog out. This was going to be more fun than he thought. If he wanted to, he could just walk in and grab her. Only now he didn't have to. Now he could really have some fun. He waited . . . waited until the dog wandered to the back of the yard . . . close to the woods.

"Eenie-meanie-minie-moe." He laughed. "Looks like she's the next to go . . . "

Avon Books are available at special quantity discounts for bulk purchases for sales promotions, premiums, fund raising or educational use. Special books, or book excerpts, can also be created to fit specific needs.

For details write or telephone the office of the Director of Special Markets, Avon Books, Dept. FP, 1350 Avenue of the Americas, New York, New York 10019, 1-800-238-0658.

PROPERTY OF HILLEL ACADEMY

IF HE HOLLERS

A.G. CASCONE

If you purchased this book without a cover, you should be aware that this book is stolen property. It was reported as "unsold and destroyed" to the publisher, and neither the author nor the publisher has received any payment for this "stripped book."

IF HE HOLLERS is an original publication of Avon Books. This work has never before appeared in book form.

AVON BOOKS
A division of
The Hearst Corporation
1350 Avenue of the Americas
New York, New York 10019

Copyright © 1995 by Gina and Annette Cascone
Published by arrangement with the authors
Library of Congress Catalog Card Number: 95-94495
ISBN: 0-380-77753-3
RL: 6.7

All rights reserved, which includes the right to reproduce this book or portions thereof in any form whatsoever except as provided by the U.S. Copyright Law. For information address Avon Books.

First Avon Flare Printing: December 1995

AVON FLARE TRADEMARK REG. U.S. PAT. OFF. AND IN OTHER COUNTRIES, MARCA REGISTRADA, HECHO EN U.S.A.

Printed in the U.S.A.

RA 10 9 8 7 6 5 4 3 2

For Peter P. Cascone, Jr.
who taught his children to follow
their dreams . . .
and always made that possible

1

He was watching them from the woods behind the Pattersons' house. What incredible luck to find them all still together after so many years. Ten years, and they all still lived in the same houses, went to the same school. Ten years of believing they were safe and comfortable, out of his reach. Ten years of taking their pathetic lives for granted. Ten years of thinking about nothing but themselves. What a pity. They should have been thinking about him. Because for ten years, he'd been thinking about them. And now he was back. Back in the woods. Back where it all started.

Nothing much had changed. Stacey Patterson's seventeenth birthday party looked a whole lot like her seventh. Only instead of a pony in the driveway, there were lots of a brand-new cars. And there were a few new faces. But for the most part, they were all there. All of them unaware that they were being watched . . . again.

For now, they were safe. Most of them were on the patio where the food was being served, except for a couple of jocks who were hanging by the pool. But it was early. The party was just beginning. And he was sure that as the night wore on, as it got darker, at least a few of them would be foolish enough to wander into the woods. They had forgotten all about him. Forgotten about the one, split second it takes to disappear . . . just like little Bobby Crawford disappeared. Ten years was a long time to stay scared.

He wondered if any of them ever even thought about Bobby anymore. Poor, stupid little Bobby. If he hadn't been such a spoiled, little brat, it never would have happened. He might have been allowed to grow up with the rest of them. And he might have had his own seventeenth birthday party and his own brand-new car, too. But little Bobby was selfish. And bad things happen to selfish, little children. And now, little Bobby no longer existed. What a pity.

Up on the patio, the birthday girl laughed. It could just as easily have been Stacey Patterson who disappeared ten years ago. Or any of the others who really were just as spoiled and just as selfish as Bobby. His gaze moved from Stacey Patterson to Eric Knight to Phil Richards. ''Eenie-meanie-minie-moe.'' He laughed to himself, savoring his plan. ''Who will be the next to go?''

This was going to be a blast. He had waited way too long for this opportunity. And now that he actually was there, seeing them together again, it was more exciting than he ever had imagined.

His heart raced at the sight of Mary Ellen Taylor. *Mel.* She was the prettiest little girl he'd ever seen. And now that she was all grown up, she was stunning.

He watched as she stepped out onto the patio, watched the guys watching her. Was it his imagination, or did she look toward the woods, directly toward him? What would she do if she knew he was there . . . in the woods again. For a split second, he heard the screaming in his head. Mel's screaming. And he remembered the terror on her face the last time she saw him there. But she didn't run. How amazing that was. She just stood there, screaming and screaming. Screaming for Bobby. Poor, stupid, little Bobby.

It would be different for Mel. He had very special plans for her. As long as she was as sweet and as innocent as she appeared, everything would be fine. He would love her and keep her forever. And in time, he would make her love him, too.

2

This would be the last party they ever had at the Pattersons' house. Right after graduation, the Pattersons were moving. Mr. Patterson was offered a job on the West Coast. In another two months, Stacey would be lying on the beach in Malibu—California dreamin'. But for Mel, it seemed more like a nightmare. And she knew that deep down inside, Stacey felt the same way.

They tried not to talk about being separated, and Mel couldn't imagine it. She couldn't remember a time when Stacey hadn't been a part of her life. Mel's mother said that she could still picture the two girls coming out of their nursery school together, hand in hand. She said they reminded her of those magnetic dogs: Mel with her dark hair and dark eyes, and Stacey, blond and blue-eyed.

Stacey looked like a California girl. And Stacey always talked about someday living in California. Now, "someday" was almost here and it didn't seem like such a good idea anymore. "Someday" was only good when it was a faraway dream. But now that it was approaching at the speed of light, it was the rest of their lives that seemed like a faraway dream.

"Remember the time . . ." three people said at once, snapping Mel back to the present. They'd been sitting around the picnic table, eating burgers and talking about the good old days. It was like turning pages in a scrapbook.

"Remember the time," Phil Richards went on, "Stacey's parents went away and left her grandfather in charge?"

"That was the best," Eric Knight laughed. "Whatever made him think that taking a bunch of five-year-olds to Dairy Barn was a good idea?"

"Dairy Barn was a good idea," Phil chided. "It was letting us order anything we wanted that was a problem."

"Oh, look who's talking," Stacey laughed.

"Yeah, really," Eric jumped back in. "Mr. super-duper double sundae over here, who had to have five different flavors with five different toppings."

"Plus two scoops of walnuts and a cup of sprinkles on the side," Stacey reminded them. "Just so he could have sprinkles with every bite."

"At least I wasn't the one who puked up all over Pop's car," Phil shot back.

"No, but you left one hell of a mess on my mother's new carpet." Stacey cracked up. And the rest of them laughed, too.

"I think she still hates me for that," Phil said.

"No. But she still hates my grandfather for it." They all laughed even harder.

"We really have had great times together." It came out sounding too sad. And Mel was embarrassed. She didn't want to be morose on Stacey's birthday.

"Oh, come on." Phil put his arm around her. "We're still gonna have great times together. We're all invited to California. Think how much fun that'll be."

"And I'll be back here to visit, too. A lot. My parents promised. They even said that after they're all settled, and after my freshman year, they'd think about letting me transfer to college back here."

Mel knew the chances of that happening were really slim. Mr. and Mrs. Patterson were always promising Stacey things they never intended to deliver. Even when she was little. Just so she wouldn't get upset. Just so they could hold off the theatrics that always accompanied Stacey's displeasure. Of course, that tactic always ended up backfiring, always ended up in a bigger production than if they'd told her the truth straight out. And this time, Mel was sure that the truth was that there was no way they'd let Stacey go to school 3,000 miles away from them. Even Wayne, Stacey's older brother was only allowed to go to a college within a reasonable driving distance from home. And the Pattersons already had made arrangements for Wayne to transfer to a university on the West Coast.

The sadness was beginning to take hold.

"It won't be the same," Eric said. "I'm going to miss you so much. I wish your parents had told you about moving sooner, I would have applied to a college out there."

"You know your parents wouldn't let you." Stacey stated what Eric already knew. They had been over it a thousand times.

Mel felt almost as sorry for Eric as she felt for herself. Eric and Stacey had been friends all their lives, but last year they'd started dating. Stacey was between boyfriends when the girl Eric had been seeing dumped him for another guy. It started out as Stacey consoling Eric. But it got real serious, real fast. And both Stacey and Eric claimed it was the perfect relationship, that they should have seen it all along. Who better to be involved with than a good friend, someone you've always liked and trusted?

Every once in a while, particularly right after Stacey and Eric got together, Mel thought about what it would be like if the same thing happened between her and Phil. If she made a list of qualities for the ideal boyfriend, Phil would have to score at least nine out of ten. And the times they had gone out together, pretending to be a couple because neither one of them wanted to bring a real date, she always had a wonderful time. And there were always moments when it definitely felt like they weren't pretending. But Mel could barely admit that to herself. And she would never, ever suggest it to Phil. Their friendship was too good. And even if she wanted to go out with Phil, she'd be too afraid that it would ruin what they had. Next to Stacey, Phil was her very best friend. And she couldn't stand the thought of ever losing him. Besides, now there was Jimmy. And while she had only been seeing him for a couple of months, it already felt very right. With Stacey leaving, she was going to need to know that she still had Phil. That he would always be there.

"We're all going to miss you," Phil said sincerely.

"Not as much as I'll miss you guys." Stacey meant it. "And this place. You know, this is the only house I've ever lived in."

"It's going to be so weird not coming here anymore." Stacey's house was like a second home to Mel. She never even knocked on the door anymore. She was treated just like family. And Stacey was treated the same way at the Taylor house. This was going to be like losing a sister.

"Hey, Stacey," one of the jocks called from out on the lawn where a volleyball game was under way. "Where's Wayne? I thought you said he was coming."

"He'll be here," Stacey called back.

"He was supposed to get home from college last night," Eric informed the rest of the group.

"My parents are furious," Stacey told them. "He hasn't even called yet. But I'm sure he'll be here. There's no way he'd miss my birthday."

Mel didn't believe that for one minute. None of them did. Wayne was always disappointing Stacey. And everyone else for that matter. He probably was off partying somewhere else. Or recovering from another party. This wasn't the first time that Wayne didn't show up when he was supposed to. In the past year, while he was living away from home, there were times when Wayne would disappear for days on end. And the best part was how he copped an attitude any time anyone would try to call him on it. Especially his parents. There was no question about it, Wayne easily was the most irresponsible person Mel had ever known. He always had been.

"If I were you, Stacey, I wouldn't hold my breath waiting for Wayne." Phil knew Wayne as well as the rest of them. "He probably found something better to do and just forgot."

"Thanks, Phil," Stacey said sarcastically.

"Oh, come on, Stacey," Phil said. He felt bad. "You know what I mean."

"Yeah, I know what you mean. Wayne's a screwup, right?" Stacey was always overly defensive when it came to Wayne.

"Come on, Stacey." Mel knew where it was going and she wanted to stop it. "Phil didn't say that. He just wants you to have a good time without worrying about Wayne. That's all."

"This is turning out to be the birthday from hell." Stacey was beginning to feel sorry for herself.

Mel was on her feet. "Oh no you don't." She pulled Stacey up, too. "We're going to turn this party around fast. Come on, you guys." She gestured to Phil and Eric. "Let's get things going." Mel turned the music up. Way up. And more than anything, she tried to fight back the memory that was beginning to surface. The memory of the year that Stacey really did have the birthday from hell.

3

The woods were getting dark and he was beginning to feel more and more at home. It wasn't at all like the last time.

"Hey, Stacey, where's Wayne?" It was the only thing he had been able to hear clearly the whole time he'd been watching them. "Where's Wayne?" Now that was a really funny story. Too bad he couldn't tell them. Better yet, too bad he couldn't show them. Wayne would have made such a wonderful birthday surprise.

Poor Wayne. He definitely would not be making the party. But that was his own fault. Wayne was stupid. And bad things happen to stupid, little children . . . even if they manage to grow up.

Why, why, why did they have to bring up Wayne? It really irritated him. He should have been thinking better. He should have known that Wayne had had too much to drink. He should have waited. He should have sobered him up. How could he have made such a stupid mistake? Wayne didn't even know what was happening. That was no fun at all. And now, it was too late. And Wayne got away without having to remember.

One thing was absolutely certain, he would not make the same mistake twice. He never did. The price for making even one, little mistake was way too high. He'd spent ten long years learning that. Mistakes attracted attention. And attention was no good.

The idea was to be anonymous. To blend in. That was the only way to survive. You had to lay low. You had to fit in so well that no one would even question who you were or what you were doing. And Sonny Gilman was a survivor. So was Gary Gates . . . and Ray Jones . . . and all the other names he'd used over the past ten years.

It was easy really. Most people were so naive, so unsuspecting, so gullible. And the ones who weren't, usually never bothered with you anyway. Most people didn't like to get involved . . . even if they thought somebody was being hurt. The fact was that if you were smart enough, and cool enough, you could get away with almost anything . . . even murder.

The sound of someone screaming drew his immediate attention. He knew it was Mel. He'd heard that scream so many times in his head that there was no mistaking the sound of her voice. Only this time it wasn't in his head. It was real. He strained to see what was happening. Everyone seemed to be gathered by the pool. And the dog was barking. That stupid, old retriever. He was surprised that the dog still was alive. But he couldn't concern himself with the dog. He was too worried about Mel. He couldn't see her. Why was she screaming?

He had to stop himself from rushing out of the woods right into the Pattersons' backyard. What if something happened to Mel? Everything would be ruined. Why hadn't he been paying attention? Bad things happen when you don't pay attention.

He saw a burst of water splash over the crowd. His heart was pounding. Why were they all laughing? What was happening? Where was she? Why couldn't he see her?

As some of the group started moving away, he caught sight of her. She was in the pool. With him. With Phil Richards. He hated Phil Richards. He hated them all. All but Mel.

Why was she laughing? Wasn't she mad? She should have been mad. It was too cold to be in the pool. It wasn't summer yet. You don't go in the pool unless it's summer. Those were the rules. And now all her pretty clothes were ruined. And her hair was ruined. Why was she being so nice to Phil? He would just have to teach her that there were some people that just didn't deserve being nice to.

He felt sick inside as he watched Mel and Phil playing around in the pool. Why was *he* touching her? Nobody was allowed to touch her. Nobody but him.

He had to stop watching. He had to get out of the woods. He couldn't let his emotions overwhelm him. You make too many mistakes that way. Besides, it was getting late. And there still were a lot of things he had to do.

"Just a little longer," he promised himself.

"Eenie-meanie-minie-moe." He took one, last look at them. "One by one you all will go."

He made his way back through the woods, careful of every step he took. He even remembered the shortcut out to the other side. The side the gravel road was on. The side that nobody ever payed much attention to. The side that, even now, was for the most part, deserted. The side where he had left the car. The car that had taken little Bobby away . . . ten years ago today.

4

Jimmy Baxter arrived at exactly 9:15. The first thing Mel did when she saw him come into the backyard was check her watch, and laugh when she saw the time. He told her that he got out of work at 9 o'clock and that he would be there by 9:15. He was there on the dot. He always was. She didn't know how he did it. Mr. Punctuality. It had become a joke between them. She'd even started watching out the window when he was supposed to pick her up to make sure he didn't sit outside and wait for the exact moment before he came to the door. But he didn't. His car actually would pull up in front of her house at the exact time he told her he would be there. Her parents were so impressed. Not only did he arrive when he was expected, he always had her home when she was supposed to be. It was just another reason that her parents liked Jimmy.

Everybody seemed to like Jimmy. It was impossible not to. He could talk to anybody about anything. Mel had quickly discovered that the secret to this was that Jimmy didn't really do a lot of talking; he was just a great listener. He was interested in everything and everybody. Especially her.

She saw him break into a smile when he spotted her walking across the lawn to meet him. He had a perfect smile. He could do toothpaste commercials. And jeans commercials, the ones where all the guys are on the beach barechested. And shampoo commercials; Jimmy never had a bad hair day. Stacey was jealous of Jimmy's hair. No matter how much lemon juice or "sun-in" she put on hers, she couldn't get it as perfectly blond as Jimmy's hair was.

Every time Mel saw him, she was blown away by his good looks. He was the only guy she ever dated who looked better in person than he did in her imagination.

"Am I on time?" He grinned devilishly.

Mel just smiled and shook her head.

"What happened to you?" Jimmy said, reacting to Mel's still-wet hair and the oversized sweatshirt and baggy shorts she was wearing that obviously didn't belong to her.

"Phil. Every birthday party Stacey's ever had, Phil ends up throwing me in the pool. It's practically a tradition. Why, do I look that bad?"

"You couldn't look bad even if you tried." Jimmy kissed her softly and very quickly. He knew that she was shy when it came to showing any kind of physical affection in public.

"What's that?" She pointed to the badly wrapped package he had in his hand.

"Nothing really. Just a little birthday present for Stacey."

"That's so nice," she said. "But Stacey didn't

expect you to get her anything. You barely even know her.''

"I know, but I just didn't think it was right to come empty-handed."

"What is it?'' Mel said.

"It's a copy of that stupid movie she keeps renting. It's used and I get a discount for working at the video store, so really it's nothing."

"You're so sweet." Mel kissed him on the cheek.

He put a hand to his cheek, trying to look shocked that she'd actually done that.

"Very funny."

"How 'bout we sneak off into the woods so I can get a real kiss." He took her by the wrist and pulled her toward the woods.

"No, stop it,'' Mel said a little too firmly as she pulled away. She immediately felt stupid for overreacting.

"Sorry." Jimmy stepped back, looking hurt and dejected.

"No, I'm sorry." Mel knew she'd hurt Jimmy's feelings and that was the last thing she wanted to do.

"What's the matter; don't you want to kiss me?"

"No, it's not that. It's just . . . I don't know. I just don't like the woods."

He didn't say anything, but his eyes were full of questions. He knew something was upsetting her and he wanted to hear what it was.

But Mel didn't really want to talk about it. "Something terrible happened in these woods"—she tried to shrug it off—"a long time ago."

"To you?" His face was full of concern.

"No, not to me." Mel was uncomfortable. "A little boy got kidnapped back here. I saw it happen, but I couldn't stop it. There was nothing I could do."

That was what they all told her; that she couldn't possibly have done anything to stop it. It was what her parents said, and the police, and the psychologist her parents took her to to help her get over it. Even Bobby's parents told her that.

Intellectually, she knew it was true. But even now, she couldn't help feeling guilty that she didn't go after him. Sometimes she'd play it over in her mind wondering if she could have gotten Bobby away from that monster.

"Poor Mel." He put his arms around her and held her protectively. "That's so terrible."

"No," she sighed, remembering what she'd tried so hard to forget. "Poor Bobby."

"The little boy?"

She nodded. "Bobby Crawford."

"Did they ever find him?"

"No. The police thought the kidnapper would try to get a ransom because Bobby's parents had a lot of money. But nobody ever contacted them. Bobby just disappeared."

"That must have been hard on the parents."

"It killed them both."

"I can imagine," he said.

"No," Mel said, knowing that Jimmy didn't understand what she was really saying. "It literally killed them."

"You're kidding, right?" Jimmy was taken aback.

"No. His parents were a lot older than most parents when Bobby was born. And his father had heart problems to begin with. A couple of months after Bobby was kidnapped, his father had a heart attack and died. And his mother couldn't go on. First she lost her only child, then her husband. One day she just took a bottle full of sleeping pills. And that was it. The whole family wiped out. It's the worst thing that's ever happened around here."

Jimmy didn't say anything.

"Sad, huh?" Mel broke the silence.

"More than sad," he said quietly, gravely.

And Mel was touched by how sensitive Jimmy was.

"What was the kid doing in the woods in the first place?" he asked.

"He was looking for his baseball."

"Why is it that terrible things always seem to happen over something so simple?"

"I don't know," Mel said, just to say something.

But it wasn't simple at all. It was the part of the story that she never told, not even to the police. It was the part of the story that still haunted her—the part of the story that still haunted them all.

5

Mel saw the squad car parked in front of the Pattersons' house the minute she turned onto the street. The mere sight of it was enough to throw her into a panic. The police never showed up with good news. Never. The police only came if there was an emergency, or a tragedy . . . or a kidnapping.

Mel's heart was pounding so hard, she could barely catch her breath. One horrible thought after another raced through her head. And every one of them centered around Wayne. *What if they were all wrong? What if something terrible really did happen? What if he really was missing? Or hurt? Or dead?*

In the past week, no one had taken Wayne's disappearance seriously. Not even the Pattersons. They pretty much were accustomed to the fact that both Wayne and Stacey were famous for pulling the disappearing act every time they were in trouble, or wanted to make some.

When they were young, Wayne and Stacey used to "run away from home" together almost every other day. Only back then, they never ran very far. Most of the time, they hid out in a neighbor's backyard just long enough to panic their parents into calling the police. But as Wayne and Stacey got older, they got much more imaginative. And while Wayne definitely was the bigger offender—taking off for weeks at a time with all kinds of crazy characters, to all kinds of crazy places—Stacey had managed to pull a couple of wild stunts of her own. In the past two years, Stacey's parents had twice reported her missing. Once when she checked into a hotel during a school night, just to torture them into thinking that she really had run away; and once when she hid out at her grandfather's house for the weekend while he was out of town.

Consequently, Stacey's parents were a whole lot less worried about Wayne's disappearance than they were pissed about it. Even the missing-persons report the Pattersons filed with the police, two days after Stacey's birthday, had little to do with concern. In fact, Stacey claimed that the only reason that her father even filed the report was just to scare the daylights out of Wayne. Just to teach him a lesson. Just to make sure that before Wayne ever took off again without consulting them, he'd think twice.

Everybody thought the whole thing was pretty funny, particularly Eric and Phil who were dying to see the look on Wayne's face the minute he realized that his father had the entire police force out looking for him. And even Stacey had to crack up when Eric suggested sticking Wayne's picture to every milk carton in every 7-Eleven in the state, just so Wayne would get the message. It really was funny, because none of them thought, not even for a second, that something bad might have happened to him.

Until now. Now it was all Mel could think about as she turned past the police car into the Pattersons' driveway. She sat there with the motor running, wondering what to do. She was supposed to pick up Stacey to go to the mall in their never-ending search to find dresses for the prom. But now it looked like that was out of the question.

The front door opened and two policemen came out and headed down the walkway back to the squad car. They didn't look particularly solemn to Mel. In fact, it looked as though both of them were pretty amused about something. They certainly didn't look like the bearers of bad news. Maybe they'd found Wayne. Maybe everything was all right.

Mel turned off the engine and got out of the car as the police car pulled away from the curb. As she headed toward the house, she heard voices, loud voices, angry voices.

"This is the last straw." Mr. Patterson's voice carried. "That boy will never get another penny from me as long as he lives. If he wants to go to college, he can find a way to pay for it himself."

The police must have found Wayne. And obviously he was safe . . . at least until he got home. Mel turned around and headed back toward the car. The last thing she wanted to do was get involved in whatever was going on inside.

"Mel," Stacey called after her.

Mel turned to see Stacey running toward the car.

"Get me out of here." Stacey got into the passenger side.

"What's going on?" Mel said as she pulled out of the driveway.

"You're not going to believe what Wayne did this time."

"The way your father was screaming, it must be big."

"Oh, it's big all right. For starters, he skipped all his exams. That means he doesn't get credit for any of his courses this semester. Which means that my father spent all that money for nothing."

"No wonder he's furious." Mel thought he had every right to be mad.

"But that's not the best part. Wanna guess where Wayne is right now?"

"Jail?" It popped out of Mel's mouth without ever registering in her brain. And when she heard what she'd said she had to laugh.

Stacey laughed too. "If my father has his way, that's next. No. Get this. Wayne is in the Bahamas."

"You're kidding me." Mel had to fight to keep her attention on the road.

"I wish. One of the things the police checked for was activity on Wayne's credit card, the one my parents gave him to use for emergencies. And they found out that he charged a round-trip ticket to the Bahamas and took a big cash advance."

"No way." Mel shook her head in disbelief. This was way out there, even for Wayne. "Well I guess you've got to do something if you're going to skip exams. So when is he coming back?"

"According to the ticket, like two weeks from Friday."

"How could he do this to your parents?" The minute she said it, Mel realized that Stacey would be offended by the fact that Mel was sounding critical of Wayne. She was right.

"Look at what my parents did to him," Stacey said defensively. "To both of us for that matter. They decided to drag us all the way across the country without even asking us how we felt about it. If you look at it from Wayne's point of view, what was the point of taking his exams when they were making him transfer out anyway. If Wayne were smart, he'd never come back. And if I were smart, I'd buy a plane ticket and join him."

Mel shot Stacey a look.

"I should, you know," Stacey said, contemplating the idea. "Maybe then they'd get the message."

"You can't be serious?" Mel said, hoping that Stacey wasn't, but knowing that there was a good possibility that she was.

Stacey smiled coyly.

"Oh, no." Mel shook her head. "You are not running away to the Bahamas." Mel issued the statement like a parent delivering an ultimatum.

"Don't panic." Stacey blew off Mel's concern. "I probably don't have enough money anyway."

It hardly was the reassurance Mel was hoping to hear.

"And I really doubt that my father would be willing to lend me his credit card."

Mel had to laugh in spite of herself.

"Daddy." Stacey affected a sugary-sweet tone. "Do you mind if I borrow your credit card so I can run away to the Bahamas with Wayne? Because I really want to get the hell away from you and Mom."

"Come on, Stacey, you don't mean that."

"Yes, I do. I just can't take them anymore. You know what they're really upset about, don't you? The money. I'm telling you, it's all they care about. Even the cops couldn't believe it. They thought that my parents would be relieved to know that Wayne was safe, and probably having a real good time in the Bahamas. And instead, my father goes ballistic on the cops over how much money Wayne wasted."

Mel couldn't help laughing. Now she understood why the cops looked so amused when they came out of the house.

"What's so funny?"

"The whole thing. I'm sorry. I just can't help it." Mel was overcome with a terrible case of the giggles. So bad, that Stacey couldn't help but catch it too.

"What? What is the matter with you?" Stacey tried to sound annoyed, but she was laughing too hard.

"I'm just trying to imagine what the cops said to your parents. 'Mr. and Mrs. Patterson, we have some good news . . . and some bad news. The good news is that your son's not dead. The bad news is that he's living it up on your credit card in the Bahamas.' I wish I had seen your father's face."

"Oh, it was priceless. He looked like a cartoon character. I swear his head blew up three times its size and there was steam coming out of his ears. And you haven't even heard the best part."

"There's more?"

"The poor cop was shaking in his boots when he had to tell my father that the university filed a complaint against Wayne. I swear he had his hand on his gun."

"A complaint? About what?"

"Destruction of property. Apparently when the cops got the dean to open Wayne's dorm room for them, the place was a disaster area. Graffiti on the wall, cigarette burns everywhere, missing furniture, and a smashed window. And the dean is blaming it all on Wayne, because Wayne hasn't had a roommate since the first semester."

"Oh, my God," Mel gasped.

"Yeah, that's what my mother said just before she burst into tears and ran out of the room. According to the cop, the window alone is gonna cost them a couple of hundred bucks. And my father didn't feel a whole lot better when the cop assured him that at least the window wasn't Wayne's fault. Somebody must have been playing ball outside and accidently threw it through Wayne's window. Because there was a baseball or something on the floor with all the broken glass."

"Somebody? *Somebody* threw a ball through Wayne's window?" Mel was laughing so hard she almost missed the turn into the mall.

They looked at each other and Stacey had to admit what she knew, Mel knew.

"Probably Wayne," they said together. And laughed. Never thinking for a second that Wayne was not living it up in the Bahamas.

6

"Mission accomplished,'' Stacey said with a great sigh of relief, as she pushed open the door to leave the mall. Mel was right behind her. And after six long weeks of almost nonstop shopping, each of them finally had a dress.

Mel checked her watch. "I can't believe we've been in there four-and-a-half hours.''

"But at least this time we've got something to show for it,'' Stacey said.

They stepped off the curb and headed toward the car, which was parked all the way on the other side of the parking lot.

"Are you really, really sure about this dress, Stace?''

"How many times do I have to tell you,'' Stacey grumbled, exasperated. "I'm sure. The dress is perfect. But I still think you should have gotten those earrings. They matched the dress perfectly.''

Mel stopped walking and glanced back over her shoulder at the mall. She was tempted, very tempted.

"This is your last chance. If you want them, let's go back and get them now. 'Cause I don't want to make another trip here any time soon. I'm malled out.''

"No." Mel started walking again. "I don't need another pair of earrings." She reached into her pocket to get her car keys. They weren't there. She tried the other pocket. Nothing. "Uh-oh."

"What's wrong?"

"Hold this." Mel handed her dress to Stacey and dug through her purse—without luck. She shook the purse but didn't hear any jingling.

"You lost them." It was a statement, not a question. Stacey was used to this. For as organized and as responsible as Mel was, she had a talent for losing keys. "So, should we waste another two hours trying to retrace our steps, or should we just call somebody to come get us? You do have spare keys at home, don't you?"

"Better than that. I have a set under the bumper in a magnetic box. Jimmy put it there after the last time."

"Thank goodness for Jimmy."

When they got to the blue Grand Prix, Stacey went to the passenger side, holding the dresses, waiting for Mel to retrieve the keys from under the car. Something caught her eye. "Oh, Mel."

"Yeah." She found the keys and moved to her door.

Stacey was just standing there pointing at the ignition. "Look."

Mel did. "Oh, no. I can't believe I did that." She unlocked the door with the spare, so focused on her keys in the ignition that she didn't notice what was sitting on the seat.

"You're lucky the car wasn't stolen," Stacey scolded as she opened her door and hung the dresses in the back.

"What's this?" Mel picked up the small, gift-wrapped package that was on her seat. There was a card attatched. Her name was written in block letters on the envelope. "Did you put this on my seat?" she asked Stacey as they got into the car.

"Not me."

"Come on. It had to be you. The door was locked."

Stacey shook her head. "Sorry."

Mel opened the card. Inside, also in block letters, it said, "From your secret admirer." She showed the card to Stacey.

"It has to be Jimmy." Stacey stated the obvious.

"Who else?" Mel agreed, smiling. She scanned the parking lot, looking for him, and was disappointed that she couldn't find either Jimmy or his car.

The only other person Mel saw was a man, about as old as her father, sitting in a beat-up, old car two lanes away. His car was directly facing hers, and he appeared to be staring at her. He was a big man, more broad than tall. His stocky build was intimidating, but his face was soft and round, and his expression guileless. And while he could have been staring at Mel, his expression suggested that he could just as well have been staring off into space, daydreaming.

But there was something familiar about him. And for a moment, Mel thought he might be someone she knew, or someone she ought to remember. She had the feeling that she should smile at him, or wave, or acknowledge him in some way. She searched her memory for a clue to his identity. *Was he a friend of her parents? A teacher? Mail-*

man? Store clerk? Nothing was coming to her. And since he hadn't acknowledged her either, Mel decided that he probably was just a stranger. Still, there was something about him that held her attention.

"Are you going to open that box, or what?" Stacey prodded impatiently.

Mel looked down at the box in her hand. How she wished Jimmy were there. For Mel, there was something unfulfilling about opening a gift without the presence of the giver. It was as if the joy of it was somehow incomplete. But there was no way to explain that to Stacey. Stacey regularly tore her house apart looking for birthday and Christmas gifts. Even wrapped presents weren't safe. Stacey could open a package, look at the gift, try it on even, and put it all back so that no one would suspect it had been disturbed.

"What are you waiting for?" Stacey practically shouted.

So finally, Mel obliged by tearing off the paper and lifting the lid. She couldn't believe her eyes. Inside the box were the amethyst earrings that matched the color of her dress, the ones she'd admired but hadn't bought for herself. Wordlessly, she handed them to Stacey, who also was shocked into silence. But only for a minute. "How romantic," Stacey sighed, just a little envious. She handed the box back to Mel.

"This is unbelievable. How did he do this?"

"He must have been following us." Stacey offered the only logical explanation.

"How? I didn't see him. And even if he were

following us, how could he know I wanted these earrings?"

"Mel, everybody in the mall knew you wanted those earrings. You had your nose pressed up against the window looking at them for so long that you steamed up all the glass. I half expected the guy behind the counter to hand you a bottle of Windex and make you clean it."

"This is just too much." Mel started the car. "Do you mind if we stop by the video store on the way home? I want to go thank Jimmy right now."

"No problem," Stacey answered. "Trust me, I'm definitely in no hurry to get home."

Mel backed out of the parking space and headed off without giving another thought to the man staring at her from the beat-up, old car two lanes away.

7

Lenny Seager sat watching as Mel and Stacey pulled out. His heart was racing. And his hands were all sweaty, just like they always got when he was following someone. And as he watched Mel's car heading toward the exit two lanes ahead, he reached for one of the candy bars he had in the bag on the seat next to him. Lenny liked eating candy. It always seemed to calm him down, especially when he was trying to follow someone.

And Lenny Seager had to calm down and follow

the rules. He had to make sure that he waited before he started the car, until Mel and Stacey were a safe distance away. And he had to make sure that they didn't turn around, that they didn't look back. He had to be careful. He wasn't even going to touch the key in the ignition until he was sure that he saw Mel's car turn out of the parking lot. There was no room for mistakes. Mistakes attracted attention. And attention was no good.

Those were the rules . . . at least when you were following someone. You were never, ever supposed to give the person you were following any reason to suspect that they were being followed. And no matter how much you wanted to, you couldn't start the car up right away . . . and pull out real fast . . . and tail them real close. Because that was the way you got seen. That was the way you got caught. And only a moron would follow someone like that. So Lenny Seager waited, just like he was supposed to.

There were rules for everything. Rules you learned to follow. Rules you didn't break. You just had to be smart enough to keep them straight. Because the rules weren't always the same, especially when you were driving.

Like waiting. You only had to wait when you were following someone. But when you were gonna rob 'em . . . like in a gas station . . . or a liquor store . . . or something like that . . . you never waited. You always had to make sure to start the car up right away . . . and pull out real fast. Because that was the only way you *didn't* get seen, the only way you *didn't* get caught.

Lenny liked robbery . . . almost as much as he

liked kidnapping. Because of the driving. You always got to go real fast. And while kidnapping was a lot more fun, robbery was a whole lot easier, because everything else before the driving was a whole lot easier to remember.

There wasn't a lot you had to think about. Like making up names. You never had to do that. In fact, you weren't supposed to give any name at all. And the best part about robbery was that you didn't even have to pretend that you weren't going to take the money. You could just walk right in, hold up the gun, say "give me the money," and walk right out. Yeah. Robbery was a piece of cake . . . even for a moron.

But kidnapping . . . that was real tricky. You had to do all kinds of thinking. And you always had to make up a name, a real good name, one that wasn't hard to remember. And you always had to pretend like you weren't going to take the kid . . . at least in the beginning. You had to watch. And you had to wait . . . until you were sure that you could grab one . . . without being seen.

Lenny saw Mel's car turn the corner out of the parking lot. And as he reached for the key in the ignition, his mind flashed back to the woods . . . back to the day he got Bobby . . . back to the day he first saw Mel.

8

When Stacey and Mel walked into the video store, Jimmy was up on a ladder hanging a poster for a movie that neither one of them had ever heard of.

"What are you doing here?" He smiled his perfect smile as he came down the ladder.

"I came to say thank you." She wanted to kiss him, but that would have to wait until later when he got out of work.

"Thank you? For what? Being such a great guy," he joked and winked at Stacey.

"For being my 'secret admirer.' "

"That's no secret. Hey, Mark," he called to the young guy behind the counter. "See this girl? I'm crazy about her."

Mark smiled and shook his head. Mel smiled back at him, embarrassed.

"See?" Jimmy teased.

"You are so weird." Stacey poked him.

"I meant," Mel said, reaching into her pocket, "thank you for these." She held out the box with the earrings in it.

"What's that?"

"Don't play dumb." She opened the box. "I

know you put these earrings in my car at the mall this afternoon.''

''Mel, I wasn't anywhere near the mall today.'' He was serious.

''Good try.'' Mel grinned. ''But who else could have done it?''

''It wasn't me. I wish I had given you a present. But I didn't,'' he said almost apologetically.

''Then who did?'' Mel found that she was more concerned than curious and she didn't know why.

''A *secret* admirer,'' Stacey answered, amused. ''Maybe it's even a stranger.''

Mel flashed back to the man in the car who was staring at her in the parking lot. It was a stupid thought. Beyond paranoid. *That guy probably was just waiting to pick up somebody. All the way at the back of the parking lot?* Why was she thinking about him, anyway? ''What an awful thought.''

''What's so awful about a guy who leaves expensive presents?'' Stacey wanted to know.

''Whoever it was, was following us without our knowing that we were being followed. And he broke into my car. What if he's some kind of nutcase?''

''You've seen too many movies,'' Stacey admonished.

''I don't like it,'' Jimmy brooded.

''I'll bet you don't,'' Stacey teased playfully. ''Looks like you've got some competition.''

''Stacey, this is not a joke,'' he rebuked.

''Whoa,'' Stacey huffed, clearly offended by his tone of voice. ''Looks like the green-eyed monster just reared its ugly head.''

"You think I'm jealous?" Jimmy scowled at her.

Stacey shrugged. The answer seemed obvious.

"So you don't think there's anything wrong with the fact that someone was following Mel? That someone was in her car?"

"To leave a pair of earrings, Jimmy. Not a bomb."

"Will you two please stop it," Mel reprimanded.

"I'm sorry." Jimmy was immediately contrite. "Really. Stacey, I shouldn't have spoken to you that way."

"It's okay," Stacey assured him. She was quick to anger, but she also was quick to let it go.

"Do you really think I should be worried about this?" Mel asked Jimmy.

"No," he answered, not entirely convincingly. "Stacey's right. I was just reacting like a jealous boyfriend. I don't like the idea of somebody else leaving you presents. But I guess leaving a present for a pretty girl doesn't make a guy a psychopath."

"Maybe not. But my mother taught me never to take anything from strangers." Mel walked over to the trash can and dropped the earrings in. "Better safe than sorry."

"What are you doing?" Stacey gasped.

"If they're not from Jimmy, I don't want them."

"Really?" he beamed.

"Really." Mel meant it.

"Well you can't just throw jewelry in the garbage." Stacey retrieved the box. "If you don't want them, I'll keep them. I don't have a problem accepting gifts from a secret admirer. Even if he's not mine. And even if he is a psychopath."

* * *

From the beat-up old car, parked across the street from the video store, Lenny Seager watched . . . and waited.

9

Stacey's parents left the house that night without even bothering to say good-bye. They always did that when they were angry. And this time they were livid. They took away her phone. They took away her car keys. And if they hadn't had to go to some stupid dinner party, they probably would have been able to take away the last little piece of sanity she had left. They'd gotten awfully close.

Stacey was lying on her bed in the dark when she heard the front door close. She wasn't crying anymore. She was long past crying. Now she was vibrating with rage.

Satisfied that her parents were gone, Stacey left her room and headed downstairs to the kitchen. She snatched the phone off the wall on her way to the refrigerator and dialed Mel's number. While she waited for Mel to pick up, she opened the freezer door and pulled out a pint of chocolate fudge-brownie ice cream and a pint of chocolate-chip cookie-dough ice cream, too. She had to maneuver around Butkus, the old retriever who was sleeping in the middle of the kitchen floor.

"Hello." Mel's voice came over the line as Stacey pulled the lid off the first pint.

"Mel?"

"Hiya, Stace. What's up?"

"I've got to get out of here."

"Why? What happened now?"

"My parents are insane. That's what happened now." Stacey shoveled a spoonful of ice cream into her mouth. "I'm telling you, they're totally unreasonable. And they're getting worse by the day. I swear to God, I'm just gonna take off and never come back."

"Come on, Stace, you don't mean that." Mel tried to pacify her. She'd been through this routine a number of times.

"Oh, no?" Stacey kept shoveling the ice cream as she talked. "Just watch me."

"Why don't you just calm down and tell me what happened, okay?"

"Mr. Fowler sent a warning note home. And my parents snapped out on me."

"Mr. Fowler? The Health teacher?"

"Yeah. Can you believe it? I'm pulling an 'A' in Human Physiology. I can practically perform open-heart surgery. But because this bozo, Fowler, doesn't think I have a good attitude, my parents go berserk."

"What do you mean, berserk?"

"Berserk. Screaming at me like maniacs about how they will not allow me to turn out like Wayne."

Butkus lumbered to his feet and begged for food.

"I'm sure it'll blow over. It always does," Mel consoled.

"Get off me," Stacey screamed when Butkus jumped up on her to get some ice cream.

"What?"

"The stupid dog," Stacey told Mel as she shoved Butkus with all her might. "Go lay down," she hollered at him. But it did no good.

"Stace, there's no point in screaming at him." Mel tried to calm her. "The poor old guy can't hear a thing."

"I hate this dog." Butkus had become the object of Stacey's anger. "Here," she growled at the dog, dumping a spoonful of ice cream onto the floor. "Have a party."

The dog lapped happily at the ice cream.

"So, you wanna hear the big news of the night?" Stacey ate another spoonful of ice cream and dropped another onto the floor.

"I'm almost afraid to ask," Mel answered.

"My father says that he is not paying for either Wayne or me to go to college next year."

"He can't be serious."

"Oh, he is. He said we're both going to take time off from school and get full-time jobs so that we can see what life in the real world is like. And when he's satisfied that we've learned a sense of responsibility, then he'll foot the bill for school. It's not fair, Mel. I've been busting my butt to bring home good grades. And now, just because 'Foul-breath Fowler' decides to be a jerk, they're treating me like I'm a criminal. I can't stand them."

"Your parents are under a lot of pressure." Mel tried to rationalize.

"No. I'm under a lot of pressure. They're at a party, having a real good time."

"You're all by yourself?"

"Not if you want to count Butkus as company," Stacey said sarcastically. Butkus had had his fill of ice cream and now he wanted to go out.

"Why don't you come over here," Mel suggested.

"Can't. They took my car keys."

Ever since Stacey got her license, it was unthinkable to her that she walk the block and a half to Mel's house.

"Want me to come get you?"

"I don't know."

"Come on. You just told me you wanted to get out of there."

"I meant for good," Stacey said bitterly.

"Look, I'll be there in fifteen minutes, okay?"

Stacey didn't answer.

"Do me a favor, Stacey. Just wait for me to get there before you decide to do something crazy."

"Yeah," Stacey appeased her. "Okay."

Mel hung up and Stacey stood there wondering what she really was going to do.

10

Mr. and Mrs. Patterson were making a very big mistake. And Stacey was about to pay for it.

He smiled as he popped open the can of beer he was holding and took a swig. Rule number one: Never, ever leave a child unattended. The Pattersons should have remembered that. What a pity. Some people just never learn from their mistakes.

He reached into his pocket to get a cigarette, the last one in the box. He lit it up, and tossed the empty box behind him. And as he watched Stacey . . . moving about the kitchen . . . in front of the big glass doors . . . the ones that opened up onto the patio . . . the ones that allowed him to see in so clearly . . . even from the edge of the woods . . . he was grateful . . . grateful that the Pattersons *were* making another mistake . . . just like they had with little Bobby.

Yeah, thanks to the Pattersons, taking little Bobby was a whole lot easier than it should have been. In fact, if they had just stayed outside with the birthday girl and all her little friends the way they were supposed to, taking little Bobby might have been impossible.

Kidnapping was all about mistakes . . . mistakes that other people made. And if you were smart, you knew that all you had to do was wait. And watch. And know exactly when to move. Like the day Bobby Crawford disappeared.

He took a drag off the cigarette. What a pity. Bobby wasn't even the one who was supposed to be taken. But Bobby screwed up. And the rules were the rules. Never take any chances . . . always grab the first kid you can . . . the first kid to make a mistake . . . a mistake like wandering off into the woods.

Nobody really wanted Bobby. Little girls were always better, so much more valuable. And in the beginning, Lenny would have traded Bobby in a minute for a little girl, a pretty little girl, like Mel or Stacey. But swapping kids was pretty much an impossible thing to do . . . unless you were in a nursery. So little Bobby had had to do. Besides, it didn't really matter anymore. Because he was going to have them all.

The kitchen door opened. "Get out," Stacey said loud enough for him to hear as she shoved the dog out.

Beautiful. He took a swig of the beer as he watched Stacey step back into the house and close the door. What luck. What incredible luck. He took another swig. Yeah. It was all about mistakes . . . mistakes like letting the dog out. "Eenie-meanie-minie-moe." He laughed. "Looks like Stacey's next to go."

This was going to be more fun than he thought. Now he wouldn't have to go into the house, even though the Pattersons had made that a fairly easy thing to do. In fact, if he wanted to, he could just walk in and grab her . . . pull it off the same way as a robbery. Only now he didn't have to. Now he could really have some fun.

He downed the rest of the beer, crushed the can, and tossed it behind him, back into the woods, near the spot where little Bobby disappeared. And he waited . . . waited until the dog wandered to the back of the yard . . . close to the woods.

"Butkus," he said as he stepped out onto the lawn right in front of the dog. "How ya doin', boy?" Butkus started to back up, started to show his teeth, the ones that were left. "It's okay, boy." He reached into his shirt pocket for the candy bar, the one he was saving, the one he almost ate in the car. "See?" He broke off a piece and held it out to Butkus. "Look what I have for you here."

Butkus sniffed the candy. Then he took it.

"Good boy, Butkus." He patted Butkus on the head. "Good boy. You want some more?"

Butkus wagged his tail.

"Come on." He moved back toward the woods and Butkus followed. "Here you go." He broke off another piece.

And once he got Butkus where he wanted him, he threw the candy wrapper away, took off his gloves, and waited.

11

Stacey didn't want to wait for Mel. She wanted to take off. She wanted to disappear. Just like Wayne had. Maybe then her parents would realize what a mistake they were making. Only there was no place to go, not without a car anyway.

She dug through the kitchen drawers looking for the spare set of keys to her mother's Volvo. Wayne's keys. The ones he had made his junior year in high school right after he got his permit, but months before he got his license.

Stacey's parents hadn't even known the keys existed. And if Wayne hadn't needed a lookout, Stacey was sure that she wouldn't have known about them either.

Wayne promised Stacey that he would only take the car when their parents were out. That way, the chances of getting caught were really slim. And Stacey's only job was to sit around hoping that Wayne made it home before their parents did. But after a couple of weeks, Wayne got really brazen and started taking the car even when they were home. Then Stacey had to make sure to keep her parents inside, away from the windows, while Wayne literally would push the car out of the driveway and three quarters of the way down the block.

Stacey thought the whole thing was pretty funny. Until Wayne smashed into the pizza parlor and their parents got hit with a $2,000-dollar repair bill. Not for the car, but for the damage he did to the window in the front of the pizza parlor. Needless to say, Wayne never got to drive the Volvo again. And their parents confiscated the keys.

Stacey slammed shut the drawer. Wayne's keys were nowhere to be found. And Stacey knew it was hopeless to start digging through her mother's coat pockets. The keys were always in the kitchen. And she was sure that by now her parents were smart enough to take anything that even resembled a car key with them.

There was nothing to do but wait for Mel. And while she probably would try anyway, she knew that there would be no way to convince Mel to drop her off at an airport or a train station, or even the local bus stop for that matter, so that she could take off for a couple of days and torment her parents.

It definitely was a lost cause. Stacey was just going to have to spend the night at Mel's.

She was just about to head upstairs to grab some clothes when she remembered Butkus. He'd been out an awfully long time. And Stacey was surprised that he hadn't scratched at the door to come in. The older he got, the less time he liked to spend outside, especially when it was dark.

Stacey went over to the back door and opened it. But she didn't see Butkus anywhere.

"Butkus," she hollered, knowing that it was futile to call him. Butkus was old and deaf, and probably half blind, too. "Butkus," she shouted even louder, straining to see him in the darkness.

Finally her eyes picked him out. He was lying at the back of the property, near the trees.

"Butkus," she called him, and clapped her hands as if that would help. But the dog didn't hear her.

"Stupid, stupid dog," she barked, stomping out of the house to go get him.

She was tempted to just leave him out there. But she couldn't do that. Butkus was Wayne's dog. And if anything ever happened to him, if he wandered off and got lost, or got hit by a car, Wayne would never forgive her.

"But-kus," she snarled as if his name were two words. She was halfway across the lawn when he turned his head toward her. She stopped. "Come here!" She gestured with her arms in wide, sweeping motions. "Come here," she repeated, gesturing again. "I can't believe I've got to talk sign language to this dopey dog," she grumbled to herself. And then to him again, "Get over here!"

But instead of getting up and heading toward her as she'd hoped he would do, Butkus turned his head away.

"You are such a pain," she shrieked, stalking across the lawn toward him.

When she reached him, she shouted his name again, and roughly grabbed his collar. The dog jumped up, and sent Stacey toppling backward.

"Damn you, Butkus," she yelled as she pulled herself to her feet and started brushing herself off.

"Hey, Stacey."

Startled, Stacey turned instinctively toward the sound of the voice.

He stepped out of the woods. "Think fast!"

But Stacey didn't catch the baseball that he threw at her. It hit her right in the stomach. Hard. So hard that it knocked the wind out of her.

And as she stood there, too stunned to move, he advanced, closing the distance between them in just a few strides.

''Remember Bobby Crawford?'' he sneered.

A moment later, Stacey was unconscious.

12

Mel had almost reached the Pattersons' driveway when she saw the car turn the corner at the end of the block onto the street. The car was old and beat-up. And it had taken the turn so quickly, that Mel could hear the tires screech.

What a jerk, she thought as she watched the car racing toward her. She steered closer to the curb to leave plenty of distance between them. She hated reckless drivers, was afraid of them. And whoever was behind the wheel of the car that was speeding toward her definitely was being reckless. By the time the car passed, Mel was sure that it was doing at least twice the twenty-five mile-an-hour speed limit that was clearly posted.

She had only managed to get a quick glance at the driver, but for a moment, she was sure that it was the very same man she'd seen in the mall parking lot. The man that was sitting in the beat-up old car, staring at her.

Mel couldn't stop her heart from pounding anymore than she could stop her imagination from running away with her. *What if it really is the same man? What if he really is some kind of psycho? And what if he is following me?* She turned around quickly to try and get another look at him. But by the time she did, the beat-up old car was already long gone.

She told herself that she was just being silly. That it couldn't possibly have been the guy from the mall. And even if it was, there was no way that he was following her, not when he came from the opposite end of the street.

Mel laughed as she took the turn into the Pattersons' driveway. "A psychopath who leaves expensive earrings," she laughed at herself. Stacey was right. She'd seen way too many horror flicks.

Mel got out of the car and headed for the Pattersons' front door. As usual, she didn't bother to knock. Stacey was expecting her anyway.

"Stace, it's me," she called as she stepped inside.

No answer.

"Stacey?" She called up the stairs toward Stacey's bedroom.

Still no answer. And since she'd noticed from outside that Stacey's bedroom was dark, she headed into the kitchen.

"Stacey, I swear to God, if you're not here, I'm gonna kill you."

Butkus was standing outside the kitchen door scratching to come in. Mel saw him and opened the door. "Hey, Butkus." She patted the big, old bear of a dog as he moved past her. "Where's Stacey, huh?" She looked at Butkus as if he might answer. But he just wagged his tail in response to the attention.

"Stacey?" Mel called out into the backyard. There was no answer. And Mel wasn't at all surprised. She didn't expect that Stacey had been outside playing with Butkus. She closed the back door and locked it. "Please don't tell me that she took off." Again she directed her comment to Butkus. It might have been hopeless, but it beat talking to herself.

Butkus's only response was to drop the ball he was carrying at her feet.

"Not now, pal, okay?" She patted his head again, and headed into the den. Butkus picked up his ball and followed her. He followed her through the entire house in her unsuccessful search for Stacey.

Finally, Mel plopped herself down on the steps in the foyer. "I'm gonna kill her."

Butkus laid down on the floor next to her, playing with his ball.

"Why does she do this? Huh?" Again she looked to Butkus for answers. "Why couldn't she have waited just fifteen minutes?"

Mel was sure that Stacey had taken off, just as she had threatened to do. And while it was odd that the doors were unlocked and Butkus was outside, considering the mood Stacey was in, Mel was sure that Stacey didn't even think about it. No, when Stacey got in one of those moods, she didn't think about anything. Or anybody.

“Poor Butkus,” Mel said, petting him playfully. “You could have been stuck outside all night, huh?”

Butkus dropped his ball on the step next to Mel, imploring her with his big, brown eyes to play with him.

“Oh no,” Mel said. “I don’t want to play with that.” She meant it. Picking up anything that Butkus had been carrying around in his mouth guaranteed a handful of slobber.

Butkus picked up the ball and dropped it again, refusing to take no for an answer.

Mel knew that he wasn’t going to give up until he had guilt-tripped her into tossing the ball at least once. “Okay,” she caved in. “But just once. Then I’ve got to go.” She picked up the ball between two fingers, trying to avoid the slobber as best she could.

The instant she reached for it, Butkus jumped up and started backing up, anticipating the toss.

But Mel wasn’t about to throw it, certainly not in the house. Because the ball that Butkus had been carrying was a baseball. And Mel hadn’t realized that until she reached for it. It struck her as being odd. Really odd. She had never seen Butkus with a baseball. He always carried a tennis ball. “I can’t throw this, Butkus.”

Butkus wagged his tail eagerly.

Mel smiled, knowing that to Butkus, a ball was just a ball. “I’ll tell you what, I’ll roll it to you, okay?” And she was about to do just that when something on the ball caught her attention.

The ball was autographed. And before Mel could stop it, the memory of Bobby Crawford surfaced, catching her totally off guard. She hadn't seen an autographed baseball since Bobby had shown her his. Mel tried to bury the memory as quickly as it had surfaced. The ball she was holding wasn't Bobby's baseball. Bobby's baseball was old, its autograph genuine. And the ball Mel had in her hand was brand new, its autograph fake and totally illegible thanks to Butkus. And Bobby's baseball disappeared ten years ago . . . with little Bobby.

Mel shook off the memory and rolled the ball across the foyer to Butkus who caught it happily, returning to drop it proudly at Mel's feet.

"Sorry, pal, I've got to go," Mel apologized as she stood up, rewarding Butkus with another pat on the head. There was no point in her waiting for Stacey. Stacey's M.O. was predictable. And one thing was certain. Stacey was not returning home, at least not tonight.

"You be good," Mel told Butkus as she backed out the front door, making sure it was locked before she closed it.

As she headed to her car, Mel hoped that Stacey had at least left a message for her at home. Even though she knew that was unlikely. In all probability, this was just the beginning of what Mel was sure was going to be another long, drawn-out ordeal.

PROPERTY OF HILLEL ACADEMY
PROPERTY O[illegible] ADEMY

13

From the moment Stacey came to she had done nothing but scream and cry and beg and plead. Exactly the way he was hoping she would. And as he listened to the noise coming from below . . . listened to her trying to kick her way out of the closet . . . knowing that the chains he'd used to shackle her legs were digging deeper and deeper into her flesh . . . causing her intolerable pain . . . he had to smile.

The chains were great, particularly now that they were old and rusted. Yeah. Beat-up, old chains always hurt a whole lot worse than shiny new ones. That was a fact. And Stacey Patterson deserved to be hurt . . . with the old chains . . . the ones he'd had for years . . . the ones that kept little Bobby under control.

Poor, stupid, little Bobby. He shook his head, amused, as he reached up into the cabinet to pull out a can of dog food. No one had ever been more petrified of the chains than little Bobby. In fact, just the mere sight of them was enough to get him to scream his little head off, like he was gonna be murdered. And as he reached for the can opener, he had to laugh. Not only at the memory of little Bobby . . . but at the idea that sooner or later he was bound to get the same reaction from Stacey . . . and all the rest of them. It was just a shame that they weren't little anymore. Little ones were so easy to terrify, so easy to train, so easy to control.

And control definitely was the name of the game. Only it wasn't really fair. Because the guy with the chains always won. He cracked up as he dumped the dog food onto a plate. Yeah. Winning control of people was a lot like taming wild horses. All you had to do was get yourself some heavy rope, or some beat-up, old chains, and tie them up real good so that you could break their spirits and get them to do anything you wanted them to do.

And once you chained them up, you had to keep them confined in a real tiny, little space so they couldn't move around much. And you wanted to keep it cold, and damp, and real dark, so that it was real scary. And the rules were that you never, ever tried to take the chains off until the screaming stopped, and the crying subsided, and the begging and pleading turned into promises of total submission.

He opened the door to the basement. "Deirdre, Deirdre, Deirdre," he said as he started down the stairs. "You're not being a very good little girl. Now are you?"

Stacey continued banging on the door.

"If you insist on acting like a spoiled little brat, I'm gonna have to treat you like one." He reached the landing and headed straight for the utility closet, where Stacey lay chained. "You know that, don't you?"

Stacey kicked at the door even harder.

"Keep it up, and your little butt will be grounded. Because I swear I'll saw your little legs off." He laughed.

Again Stacey kicked at the door.

"Is that what you want?" He kicked back at the door. "Is it?" He kicked even harder. "Because if that's what you want, I'd be more than happy to do it for you."

Stacey got quiet.

"Really. It's not a problem. In fact, it's a pretty easy thing to do, particularly with a chain saw. You know what a chain saw is, don't you?" He heard Stacey backing away from the door, or at least trying to. "They're the really big saws. You know, the ones that go vroom, vroom." He laughed maliciously. "And I bet you wouldn't even feel a thing until it was over. Because it goes so fast. I mean, really fast. Yeah, it's pretty amazing how quickly one of those things can cut through a couple of bones. So what do you say, huh?" He reached out to grab the handle on the closet door. "Should we give it a try?" He jiggled the knob. And Stacey screamed. Just like he knew she would. Just like little Bobby had. "Now, are we gonna be a good, little girl, or not?"

Stacey didn't answer.

"Deirdre, I'm talking to you."

"Why are you doing this?" Stacey screamed. "Why are you calling me that?"

He laughed. "What's the matter, Deirdre? Don't you like your new name? I picked it out just for you." He had too. He'd picked that name just because he hated it so much. Just because it was the most awful name he could think of. Next to Ernest.

The first name little Bobby learned to answer to. "It's such a pretty name. Much better than Stacey. Stacey's a stupid name. And we don't want you to have a stupid name, now do we?"

"Please," Stacey begged. "Please just let me go."

"Go where? Huh, Deirdre? Where do you want to go?" He couldn't wait to hear her answer, knowing that it would be the same one little Bobby gave, the same one they all gave.

"Home," Stacey cried pathetically. "I want to go home."

"Now why would you want to do that when we're having so much fun together?" Yeah. Being the guy with the chains was definitely a whole lot of fun. "Besides, there's nobody for you to go home to anymore. Because guess what? Your mommy and daddy are dead. I know that because I killed them."

He loved this part. The reactions were always so amusing. And while he was hoping that Stacey would throw up all over herself, just the way little Bobby had, he knew it was a long shot. She probably was smart enough to know that he was lying. After all, she wasn't seven anymore. She wouldn't be as gullible as little Bobby. Yeah, traumatizing a seventeen-year-old was much more challenging.

Stacey was silent.

"What's the matter, Deirdre? Cat got your tongue?"

Stacey didn't answer.

"Or don't you care that your mommy and daddy are dead?"

"Stop it," Stacey screamed. "Just stop it!"

"Stop it?" he mocked. "We haven't even started yet." He unlocked the door to the utility closet and opened it. "In fact," he said as he laid the plate of dog food down on the floor in front of her, "you might want to eat. Because you're definitely gonna need to keep up your strength for what I've got planned for you."

Stacey cowered in the corner.

"Go on," he said. "Eat."

Stacey didn't move.

"What's the matter? Don't you like Mighty Dog? It's really good. Tender, moist, and meaty. Just like all the commercials say it is."

Stacey didn't move.

"I said eat it!" He kicked her hard.

"I can't," Stacey whimpered. "Not with my hands chained behind my back."

"Oh." He feigned concern. "How terrible. I didn't realize. I bet if I just unchained you, then you'd eat it all up. Right?"

"Right." Stacey's voice sounded hopeful.

"Maybe I should even go upstairs and get you a fork. And a really sharp knife. Would that be helpful?"

Stacey nodded.

"Sure. That's what I'll do," he mocked sincerely. Stacey was much more gullible than he'd hoped. "And then, maybe when I knock out all your teeth, the tooth fairy will fly on in and leave you a ton of money, too." He laughed.

Stacey looked horrified.

"Now," he said as he got down on his knees. "This is the way you do it." He put his hands behind his back as if they were chained. Then he leaned forward into the dish and took a mouthful of the dog food. "See?" He chewed it up as if he were truly enjoying it. "Just like a dog."

Stacey's eyes welled up with tears. "Please. Please don't make me do this."

He grabbed her by the hair. And just as he was about to push her face into the plate, something caught his eye. "Wow." He reached for one of the earrings that Stacey was wearing, the one that was dangling from her right ear. "These are really pretty." He examined the amethyst earring as if he were seeing it for the first time. "Really pretty." He tugged on it, lightly. "I'll bet they were real expensive, too. Huh?" Again he tugged, only harder. And he smiled when Stacey winced. "It's just a shame that you can't keep them. Because they look really nice on you." He pulled the wire earring from her earlobe hard.

Stacey cried out in pain.

"You know, if I weren't such a nice guy, I'd cut your little hands off for this." He pulled the other earring out of Stacey's left earlobe. "These don't belong to you. Do they?"

Stacey shook her head, terrified.

"You stole them. Didn't you?"

"No," Stacey cried. "I didn't."

"You didn't?" he said accusingly. "Well how can that be? Tell me something, what's your name?"

Stacey didn't answer.

"What is your name?" He was becoming more agitated.

"Stacey," she answered without thinking.

He slapped her hard across the face. "Excuse me?"

"Deirdre," Stacey cried. "My name is Deirdre."

"That's right. Your name is Deirdre. And who were these earrings meant for, hmm? Were they for Deirdre? Did the card on the box say 'For Deirdre'?"

"No," Stacey answered.

"No. Of course not. The card said 'For Mel', didn't it? The card clearly said these earrings were for Mel. Isn't that right, Deirdre?"

"I only took them because Mel didn't want them."

"Yeah? Well now I'm taking them back. Because sooner or later she will." He put the earrings in his pocket. "I can promise you that." He pushed Stacey's face into the plate of dog food. "Now eat up, before I really lose my patience with you."

Stacey pulled her head back.

"Deirdre, you have two choices. Eat it. Or die."

Stacey chose to comply.

"Good girl." He patted her on the head as if she were a dog. "Just let me know when you're all finished licking the plate, so I can bring you some dessert. Like maybe a milkbone or something." He laughed as he stood up and headed for the stairs. "But don't scream, okay? It only makes me angry. Besides, there's no reason for you to scream. I can hear you perfectly through the baby monitor."

Stacey looked up at him.

He pointed to the monitor he had hanging from the basement ceiling. "I'll bet you're sorry you called me all those terrible names before. Aren't you?''

Stacey cowered in fear.

''Yeah, Deirdre, if I were you, I'd definitely think twice before I opened my filthy, little mouth again. These babies pick up everything. In fact, I can even hear you breathing.'' He took the first step. ''Oh, Deirdre.'' He turned back around. ''I was lying about your parents. They're not really dead.'' He took a dramatic pause. ''But I'll let you in on a little secret. Wayne is not in the Bahamas.''

Stacey threw up. And he smiled, satisfied.

14

''I'm gonna kill Stacey for this,'' Eric brooded as he plunked himself down in the booth at the back of the diner.

Phil slid in next to him, shooting an apologetic look across the table to Mel and Jimmy, whose Friday-night date was now a foursome.

Mel smiled back at Phil. It was okay. She knew that Phil would go crazy if he had to keep Eric occupied all by himself. Besides, Jimmy didn't mind at all. He was not the kind of boyfriend who tried to separate Mel from her friends. To the contrary, Jimmy welcomed any opportunity to get to know her friends better, to get closer to them.

''You're gonna have to take a number and get

in line,'' Mel quipped to Eric. ''I think Stacey's parents are gonna want first crack at her. And I'm next after them.''

Stacey had been gone for almost forty-eight hours and, predictably, everyone's anxiety level was rising. The Pattersons talked about filing another missing-persons report. But they hadn't done it yet. The police probably would not have taken it seriously anyway, not in light of Stacey's past behavior, and Wayne's most recent exploits.

The consensus was that Stacey was grandstanding, that she had taken off to teach her parents yet another lesson.

''I know she's trying to torture her parents,'' Eric said. ''But why couldn't she have picked up a phone and called one of us?''

''Because that would destroy the drama of it all,'' Mel explained, trying to sound more amused than she was. In fact, Mel never found it amusing when Stacey pulled stunts like this.

''And Stacey's nothing if not dramatic,'' Phil added. ''Besides, if one of us knew where she was, we'd break down and tell her parents. We wouldn't be able to let them worry like this.''

''Oh, but Stacey can let us worry,'' Eric complained. Because he was Stacey's boyfriend, he was more hurt than the rest of them that Stacey hadn't been in touch with him, and more inclined to believe that something bad had happened to her.

''There is nothing to worry about.'' Mel tried to console him.

But frustration was getting the better of Eric, and that wasn't what he wanted to hear. ''Jimmy.'' He appealed to someone who was more likely to give him the answer he was looking for. "How would you feel if Mel disappeared like this?"

"I'd probably be going crazy," Jimmy admitted reluctantly.

"Yeah, well that's exactly what I'm doing," Eric assured them, busily tearing his napkin into little pieces.

"No kidding," Phil jibed.

Mel had to stifle a smile. She knew that Phil had borne the brunt of Eric's angst. "Eric, it's not like she hasn't done this before," Mel reminded him.

"Just last summer in fact," Phil chimed in. "And she was gone even longer, remember?" To Jimmy, who hadn't been a part of the group then, hadn't even moved into town yet, he explained, "She hid at her grandfather's house while he was away on vacation. And she was gone a whole weekend before her parents figured out where she was."

"Yeah. But *I* knew where she was," Eric admitted, surprising them all.

"You did not," Mel said, unwilling to believe that Eric was capable of keeping a secret like that.

Eric nodded sheepishly.

"And you didn't tell us?" Mel shook her head like a disapproving parent. She didn't wait for an answer. "You just let us wait and worry, and all the time you made believe that you didn't know where she was either. How could you do that?"

"I had to," Eric defended himself. "Stacey made me promise her. And you know how she can be sometimes."

"And what about this time?" Phil echoed Mel's

disapproval. "Do you know where she is this time?"

"No," Eric swore, "I don't. Why do you think I'm so worried?"

"Yeah, well do us all a favor," Phil said as the waitress approached the table to take their order. "If you do hear from Stacey this time, promise you'll let the rest of us know."

"How are you guys doing tonight?" the waitress greeted them cheerily before Eric had a chance to answer Phil.

"We're doing just fine," Jimmy responded pleasantly. "How about you?"

"Can't complain. Nobody listens anyway," she kidded.

They all smiled politely at the jest. And the waitress began taking their orders.

Jimmy put his arm around Mel and pulled her just a little closer. He smiled at her, and winked, a signal to tell her that everything was okay, at least between the two of them. He was being such a good sport and Mel appreciated it. She knew that he would much rather have been alone with her. She would rather it were that way, too. And she felt a little guilty wishing that she could forget about her friends so that it could be.

15

Lenny wanted to kiss the lady in the diner . . . the lady with the menus . . . the lady who picked out the booth right in front of the big picture window . . . the window that was directly across the street from where he was parked.

Most of the time, things didn't work out so well. No, most of the time you couldn't relax at all. You'd just have to sit in the car staring at the door all night . . . wondering what was going on inside . . . and hoping that you didn't fall asleep or something . . . like a moron. No, you had to be smart. You had to follow the rules. And according to the rules . . . if you couldn't see the people you were watching . . . you weren't allowed to turn your head away from the door . . . not even for a minute. And you definitely weren't allowed to try and run out to get some doughnuts or some candy or something while you were waiting. Because the minute you stopped watching, you ran the risk of losing them. And if you lost them, you ran the risk of having to start all over again from scratch.

And, while Lenny could see all four of them clearly . . . while he knew that it definitely would be a while before any one of them got up to leave . . . he wasn't about to take any chances. No, he wasn't gonna go anywhere at all. He was gonna sit, and wait. Just in case. Because one thing was certain, Lenny Seager had no desire to start from scratch.

Just finding little Bobby's old neighborhood had been tricky enough. In fact, Lenny had driven around so many different neighborhoods . . . in so many different states . . . picking up so many different kids . . . that finding little Bobby's old neighborhood . . . ten years after the fact . . . had been the most difficult thing he'd ever done by himself.

And even though he'd been in town for a few weeks, Lenny still was having a hard time keeping his bearings straight. Yeah, the only way for Lenny *not* to screw up . . . the only way to make sure that he wouldn't have to start all over again . . . was to make sure to keep at least one of little Bobby's friends in sight . . . at all times. That way, nobody was going to get lost. And tonight, keeping an eye on little Bobby's friends was gonna be easy, at least for a little while. Because here they were, all together again. All of them . . . except Stacey.

But Lenny Seager wasn't worried about watching Stacey anymore. No, Lenny knew exactly where she was. And he was pretty sure that she wasn't going anywhere either. Not unless she was Superman or something. Lenny laughed. He liked making jokes. And that definitely was a good one. Yeah, Lenny Seager was sure that Stacey Patterson was safe and secure in the basement of 333 East Harington Street . . . the only address that he'd been able to remember so far.

It was easy. Three, three, three were Lenny's favorite numbers. In fact, he played them every day

. . . in the lottery . . . straight and boxed . . . just to make sure that no matter which way the numbers came out, he would win. The guy at the lottery machine told him that he was wasting his money, told him that the only time you played numbers boxed was when they were all different, like one, two, three. That way if they came out three, two, one, you'd still win. But three, three, three was always gonna come out the same way, no matter what. So you only had to play 'em straight. At least that was what the guy said. Only Lenny didn't believe him for a minute. No, Lenny wasn't stupid. The lottery commercial always said that if you wanted to improve your chance of winning, you always had to make sure that you played your numbers straight and boxed. So Lenny always did.

And Harington sounded a whole lot like Harry . . . Lenny's second favorite name in the whole world . . . and his first favorite life.

He reached into the glove compartment to get his wallet. Lenny liked thinking about being Harry Johnson. And he liked looking at the picture, too. While Lenny had used all kinds of names, and lived all kinds of lives, Harry Johnson's was the best.

He glanced over at the diner again, just to make sure that everything was okay. Then he pulled the stack of photo IDs out of his wallet and started flipping through them until he found the driver's license that he was looking for. The one that belonged to Harry Johnson.

It was the best picture Lenny had ever taken. And even George had to admit that Lenny didn't look like a moron at all. No, Lenny Seager looked like a million bucks as Harry Johnson. And George was pretty impressed. So impressed, that he even promised never to call Lenny, "Lenny" again.

But by the time Lenny got to be Harry Johnson, he liked being called Lenny. In fact, it was his favorite name. And even though he knew it was mean, even though he knew that the only reason George started calling him that in the first place was because he read some stupid book about a smart guy named "George" who had to look after a big stupid guy named "Lenny," Lenny didn't mind. Not really. Because Lenny told himself that it didn't matter. Yeah, Lenny told himself that no matter what George thought, or what George said, he was not a moron. And being called Lenny was a whole lot better than being called by his real name . . .

Ernest . . . Ernest Seager. Only Lenny really hated it. In fact, Lenny thought that Ernest was the most awful name in the whole world. And, as he looked through the rest of the IDs, he was grateful that there wasn't one picture of him that said Ernest under it. No, the last piece of ID that ever said Ernest on it was the fake birth certificate that George had made up for little Bobby, so that Lenny would be able to remember it easily. Yeah, little Bobby Crawford became little Ernest Johnson the very first week that Lenny got him, the very first week that Lenny got to be Harry.

Lenny's heart started racing when he glanced back over at the diner to see that the booth in front of the big picture window was empty. And he was just about to start panicking when he saw Phil and Eric step out the front door. Followed by Mel. And

. . . Jimmy. Yeah, Jimmy. That was his name. Mel, Phil, and Eric were easy to remember. He'd heard little Bobby talk about them all the time. But Jimmy . . . Jimmy was new. And it always took Lenny a little while to remember new names.

He watched Phil and Eric head to Eric's car. Lenny knew it was Eric's car because he'd been following it a lot. But he wasn't gonna follow it tonight. No, tonight he was gonna follow Jimmy's car. And even a moron couldn't miss Jimmy's car. It was a 1964 Mustang, in mint condition.

Yeah, tonight Lenny Seager was going to follow the Mustang again. Because tonight, Jimmy was with Mel. And that didn't make Lenny feel comfortable at all.

16

The note was in Eric's locker on Monday morning. It was taped inside the door. So whoever put it there had to have opened the locker, had to have known the combination. And Stacey was the only other person besides Eric who knew it.

The moment Eric saw the note, recognized Stacey's handwriting on the envelope, he was overcome with a sense of relief. It felt as though a plug had been pulled and every ounce of stress drained instantaneously from his body. For the first time in three days, his shoulders relaxed, his fists unclenched, and he could breathe normally. All he could think was that Stacey was all right. He couldn't even muster the energy to be angry with her for all that she'd put him through.

Phil and Mel were nearing the end of the hallway, heading off to their first class of the day. They'd left him only seconds before. He thought about calling to them. But he hesitated. There would be time enough later to share the news with them. Besides, the note was meant for him and he thought he was entitled to read it privately before anybody else saw it.

The first-period bell rang, and locker doors were slammed all around him as students hurried off to class. Eric hurriedly tore open the envelope, removed the single sheet of notepaper that was inside, and unfolded it.

It was a short note. And the writing was unmistakably Stacey's, though it appeared to have been scrawled in a hurry. And Eric thought that if the handwriting was any indication of Stacey's mood, it obviously hadn't improved since she left. In fact, it looked like it had gotten worse.

Dear Eric, his eyes moved right past those words and focused on the first sign of trouble. *If you really love me*, the opening sentence began. And Eric was old enough and wise enough to know that whenever anybody began a sentence that way, an unreasonable request was sure to follow. But he also knew that the sucker to whom those words were directed would probably be fool enough to comply with the unreasonable request. *Don't show this note to anyone. Don't even tell anyone else about it.* He wouldn't. Even though he was sure it was the wrong thing to do, he wouldn't go against Stacey's wishes.

Meet me tonight, the note went on, *at the end of Willow Road.* Willow Road was the dead end on the other side of the woods from Stacey's house. It was a popular make-out spot. But he and Stacey didn't go there, and he couldn't help wondering why she had chosen it as a meeting place.

I'll be there at 3 a.m.

"Not really," Eric said out loud, voicing his disbelief. Why did everything have to be such high melodrama with her? And, more importantly, why did he put up with it? He would be there. *But this was it,* he told himself, the very last time she was going to get him to do anything like this again.

Don't let anybody see you. I'll explain everything tonight. I love you. Stacey.

The hallway was nearly empty, and Eric realized that if he didn't hurry, he would be late for class. He stuffed the note into his pocket, closed his locker, and hurried down the hallway in the opposite direction that Phil and Mel had gone. He wouldn't see them again until lunchtime. And when he did, he wouldn't tell them about the note. It was a decision that bothered him, because he knew that it was the wrong thing to do.

17

"Deirdre . . . guess what time it is." He flipped on the light switch at the top of the basement stairs. "It's two o'clock." He started down the stairs. "And guess where I'm going."

Stacey didn't answer. But he could hear her crying. Just the way she had been all night.

"So, tell me something, Deirdre," he said as he opened the closet where he kept all his tools. "How much do you figure Eric weighs? Huh?" He reached up onto the top shelf to grab the bottle of chloroform. "One-sixty? One-seventy?"

Stacey still didn't answer.

"Or is he more than that?"

Still nothing from Stacey.

"You know, Deirdre, you might want to help me out a little bit here. Because if I make a mistake, Eric could end up taking a little trip to the Bahamas, too." He smiled. "And you wouldn't want that to happen, now would you?"

"I don't know how much Eric weighs," Stacey answered quickly, sounding as confused as she did frightened.

"Now that's a pity. 'Cause I'll tell you something, this chloroform stuff—you know, the stuff I used on you—well, it's pretty tricky. And knowing Eric's exact weight would make things a whole lot easier. Because if I use too little, it's definitely gonna create some problems for me. But if I use too much, there's a very good chance that it's gonna create even bigger problems for Eric." He laughed. "Yeah, if I use too much, Eric's little heart could just give out. Or, even worse, his little brain could just stop functioning. And that would be no fun at all."

That was exactly what had happened to Wayne. His little brain just cut out. And he never woke up. Only he wasn't about to tell Stacey that. Not straight out anyway. No. He wanted to milk the Wayne story for all it was worth. If nothing else, Wayne was going to provide him with a couple of laughs. "Well, let me ask you this," he continued. "Eric's not a drinker, is he?" He smiled. "I mean, like your brother. 'Cause I'll tell you what, alcohol and chloroform definitely don't mix well. Yeah, even if I manage to guess Eric's weight, if he's been drinking, the whole thing's out of my hands. I don't know, maybe I should just hit him in the head with a bat. What do you think? Would that be better?" He laughed, knowing that the night would be much more torturous for Stacey than it would be for Eric. No. He wasn't worried about Eric at all. In fact, he knew exactly what he was doing. Wayne was just an unfortunate mistake.

"Please," Stacey cried out desperately. "Please don't hurt Eric. I'll do anything you want."

"Well that's very sweet, Deirdre. Only it's ten years too late. Don't you think? Besides, you've already done everything I need you to do."

"You're never going to get away with this," Stacey sobbed.

"Oh no?" He put the bottle of chloroform in the gym bag he grabbed from the shelf. "Whatever happened to little Bobby? Huh, Deirdre? Anybody ever figure that out?"

Stacey didn't answer.

He knew she wasn't going to answer. And he didn't have the time to push it. By now, Stacey knew that anything she had to say about little Bobby only made him angry. And he was sure that she didn't want to be on the receiving end of that kind of wrath again. Nor did she want to take the chance that he would take it out on Eric. "No, no one ever found little Bobby. Did they?" And with that, he let it go. Not because he didn't want to beat the crap out of her again, but because he couldn't let his own emotions get in the way of what he had to do.

"And what are you going to do if Eric called the police or something? Huh?" Stacey was grasping at straws.

"Deirdre, Deirdre, Deirdre." He shook his head. "Your concern for me is overwhelming. But I really don't think you have anything to worry about. 'Cause we both know how much Eric loves you. Don't we? And we both know that Eric is gonna do exactly what your little note told him to do. Isn't he?"

"It wasn't my note," Stacey cried.

"You wrote it, didn't you? Poor Deirdre. You can't just wash your hands of this one. Can you?" He grabbed the rope from the closet and shoved it into the gym bag. "I told you that you didn't have to write the note. Didn't I? I gave you a choice. It's not my fault that you decided to keep your little fingers and give up Eric. Now is it?" He looked at his watch. "Look at the time."

He was cutting it close. And he knew it. It would take six minutes and forty-eight seconds to drive over to the high-school parking lot where he would leave his car. He'd timed it the night before. And it would take at least seven minutes and twenty-three seconds to walk to Willow Road. He'd also timed that the night before. If he left within the next five minutes, he'd get to the woods at just about two-thirty. And he was sure that Eric already would be waiting. Now he was going to have to enter the woods from the other side, from behind the Pattersons' house. But at two-thirty in the morning, he was sure that even that wouldn't be a problem.

He was hoping that Eric would be waiting outside of his car . . . so that all he would have to do was call to him . . . from the woods. Yeah, he definitely wanted to get Eric into the woods. Because it felt real good taking Stacey that way. And if Eric was sitting in the car, he'd have to waste a lot of time figuring out a way to attract his attention, without ruining the surprise. But one way or another, he'd get what he wanted.

Yeah, one way or another, Eric Knight was going to lose consciousness with the name Bobby Crawford echoing through his head.

And once Eric was out, he'd put him in the trunk of his own car, and drive him back to 333 East Harington Street, where a cozy little closet was all set up and ready for him. And, when he was sure that Eric was safe and secure, he'd drive back to the school parking lot, leave Eric's car, and pick up his own.

He reached into a box on the shelf, the one that had all the baseballs in it. "Guess what, Deirdre, it's showtime."

"Please," Stacey cried. "Please don't go."

He laughed. "I have to go, Deirdre. We wouldn't want to leave Eric in the woods all by himself. Now would we?"

"Please," Stacey sobbed. "Don't do this."

"That would be mean," he told her. "The woods are real scary when you're all by yourself." He headed for the stairs. "They're dark. And deep." The minute the words came out of his mouth, he smiled. "Lovely . . . dark . . . and deep," he corrected himself. It was the poem. George's poem. Only it wasn't really George's. Even Lenny knew that. Funny, he hadn't thought about that poem in years. He switched off the light and called back down. "Yeah, Deirdre, miles to go before I sleep."

18

Eric's black Camaro was already in the school parking lot when Phil pulled in on Tuesday morning. He couldn't believe it. The first thing he did was check the clock on his dashboard, to make sure he wasn't late. And he wasn't. In fact, he was right on schedule. But he should have known that just by looking around the parking lot. More than half the spaces still were empty.

But the black Camaro was there. And that wasn't just unusual, it was unheard-of. Eric never, ever arrived at school before Phil. Phil always got there first, then Mel, then Eric, and Stacey showed up last. Every day, without fail.

As he headed toward his parking space, the one right next to Eric's, he wondered why he had this sudden fixation on routine. But it wasn't sudden at all, and he knew it. Phil always had been that way, very much a creature of habit, the kind of kid who would order sprinkles on the side just so he could have the same amount with every bite of ice cream. Anal retentive, that's what Stacey always called him. And while parents and teachers referred to him as reliable, dependable, and mature, Phil couldn't help thinking that Stacey's assessment was more accurate.

There were times when Phil wished that he were less reliable, and dependable, and mature, and more like Stacey. But Phil and Stacey were as different as day and night. And he sometimes wondered, if they had not grown up together, if they had not been childhood friends, if they met for the first time now, would they even like one another.

It was a question he couldn't answer, because his relationship with Stacey was complicated. He didn't just like her, he loved her, loved her like a sister. And there was a time when it was even more complicated than that. There was a time, in their freshman year, when Stacey and Phil had dated. Nobody knew about it, not even Eric or Mel. And that was just as well because it lasted all of about a week. The same characteristics that attracted them to one another also caused the breakup. Her spontaneity made him a nervous wreck. And his sense of responsibility made her want to rebel. Fortunately, they ended the romance amicably, agreed that it never happened, and went back to being good friends.

Eric and Stacey were better suited to one another. And so were he and Mel. But that possibility had never been explored. The timing was never right. And now Mel seemed happy with Jimmy, who seemed like a nice enough guy. And the last thing he wanted to do was come between them. Besides, Phil told himself, boyfriends come and go, but the relationship he had with Mel would last all their lives.

Phil was lost in his thoughts as he parked the car and got out. He started to walk away before his brain registered what he had seen. He turned back abruptly, sure the impression was mistaken. But it wasn't. And he headed toward Eric's car to get a closer look at the damage.

The driver's-side window was shattered. Broken glass littered the interior of the car. And, laying on the front passenger's seat amid the shards of glass, was the cause of the damage. A baseball. Someone must have thrown it, or hit it, through the window. Phil couldn't imagine anyone stupid enough to be playing baseball in the school parking lot, but obviously someone had been. He only hoped that Eric never found out who it was.

Eric probably didn't even know about it yet. If he had known, he would have been out there cleaning up the glass and cursing up a storm. It looked to Phil like he was going to have to be the one to break the bad news, so he headed toward the building to look for Eric.

19

"It just doesn't make any sense," Mel said to Phil as they headed out of school at the end of the day. "Why would Eric's car be here if he's not?"

Phil just shrugged. It was a rhetorical question anyway. Because Eric's car was there. And Eric was not. Nor, it seemed, was he at home. Even if he was, he hadn't been answering the phone all day. "You want to take a ride to his house with me?"

"Sure," Mel agreed, as the two of them headed to Phil's car.

"Strange," Phil said, thinking out loud.

"What is?" she asked.

"I don't know," he answered. "It just feels as though everything is out of sync lately. You know what I mean?"

"Yeah. I feel the same way. It's like nothing's been going right since . . ." She thought about it, trying to pinpoint the exact time. "Since Stacey's birthday."

"No," Phil disagreed. "Since Stacey's parents decided to move to California."

"Hey, for all we know, Stacey's there already," Mel joked.

"I wouldn't put it past her," Phil echoed her tone, pulling out of what was sure to be a depressing conversation. "Let's just hope Eric didn't decide to join her," he added facetiously.

Mel headed around to the passenger's side of Phil's car, the side on which Eric's car was parked. She grimaced when she saw the window. Phil had told her it was broken, but this was the first time she'd seen it for herself. "Eric's gonna freak."

"That's an understatement."

"Who would do something like this?" Mel wondered out loud.

"I don't really think that anybody did this on purpose, Mel. It was probably a bunch of kids playing baseball out here, and somebody put it through Eric's window."

And for some reason, Mel found herself thinking about Wayne. And Wayne's window. What was it Stacey had said? "Somebody must have been playing ball outside and accidentally threw it through Wayne's window."

Then it caught Mel's eye. The baseball on the front seat of Eric's car. And she was jolted, not by the ball itself, but by what was written on it. "Phil," she called uneasily, her eyes glued to it. "Did you see this?"

He moved around the car toward her and peered through the broken window. "The baseball?" he asked, confused. "Of course I saw it. I told you about it, didn't I?"

"Look at it," Mel insisted.

Then Phil saw what it was that had gotten Mel's

attention. He started to reach through the window to get the ball. But there still were pieces of glass attached to the frame. So he opened the door instead, and leaned inside to pick it up. "Ted Williams," he mused as he stood staring at the signature on the ball.

And Mel knew that Phil was thinking about the very same thing she was thinking—the only other time either one of them had seen a baseball with the name Ted Williams on it. The day Bobby Crawford disappeared.

She didn't want to make that connection. She wanted to believe that it was just a coincidence. But it was too strange, and too specific to be a coincidence. And Mel was beginning to believe that what had happened to Eric's car was no accident. Then Wayne came back into her mind. She tried to stop her train of thought, tried to tell herself that it was absurd. But another picture flashed into her mind. "Butkus," she said out loud.

"Huh?" Phil was pulled out of his own thoughts.

"Butkus had a baseball." She was troubled by the realization.

"So?"

She didn't say anything. She was trying to remember, trying to picture the writing on the ball. But Butkus had been chewing on it, slobbering all over it, so that the writing had nearly been obliterated. "The night Stacey disappeared," she said to Phil, "Butkus had a baseball."

He looked at her like she was crazy.

"And somebody threw a baseball through Wayne's window."

"So what's your point?"

"What if somebody did it on purpose. What if somebody's trying to tell us something."

"You're letting your imagination run away with you," Phil said seriously. "Some kid probably just wrote it on the ball to try to fake out his friends. I used to do it with my baseball cards all the time."

"Ted Williams." Mel repeated the name to make her point.

"He was a famous baseball player, Mel." Phil tossed the ball back into Eric's car. "Come on." He opened his car door for her. "Let's go find Eric."

She hesitated, looking at the baseball. *Ted Williams.* That *was* the name on Bobby Crawford's ball. The ball that Wayne Patterson threw into the woods.

20

Lenny Seager had all that was left of little Bobby's entire life in the palm of his hand. And he knew it. In fact, it was the only thing that kept Lenny going, the only thing that allowed him any comfort at all. And as he lay down in the woods, lay down on the very same spot where Bobby Crawford's little life as he knew it came to an end, he held the ball tightly, as if he were trying to hang on to his own.

Lenny never let little Bobby's ball out of his sight. Never. And not because it was valuable either. Even though Lenny knew that it was. Yeah, George told Lenny that Bobby's baseball was real valuable. Even more valuable than little Bobby. According to George, a genuine, autographed baseball—especially one signed by a player like Ted Williams—was guaranteed to be worth a ton of money. And George was gonna try to sell it too, until he figured out that it would only cause a lot of trouble. Yeah, thanks to little Bobby's friends, the police knew all about the baseball with Ted Williams's name on it. And George knew it for a fact. Because he read about it in the paper. So if the ball was to turn up, like in a pawn shop, it was bound to create attention. And attention was no good.

George got real mad about the whole thing. So mad that he swore he was going to kill all of little Bobby's friends for screwing up the whole thing. But Lenny, Lenny wasn't mad at all. No, Lenny Seager knew that little Bobby's baseball was worth a whole lot more than cash.

He looked at his watch . . . the one he'd gotten from George . . . the one with all the timers . . . the one that took weeks to figure out. And Lenny hated it. Because no matter how hard he tried, he could never get the alarm to go off the right way. Only today, that was lucky. Yeah, today Lenny was real happy that the stupid watch went off at two o'clock in the afternoon. And not at two o'clock in the morning, the way it was supposed to. Because at two o'clock in the morning, Lenny was wide awake anyway. But at two o'clock in the afternoon, Lenny

Seager caught himself sleeping on the job, right in the middle of the high-school parking lot.

And that was a real problem, 'cause only a moron would fall asleep on the job. Yeah, only a moron would put himself in the position of being the guy who got seen, when he was supposed to be the guy doing the watching. Lenny Seager knew that. Only Lenny Seager was exhausted.

He'd been up all night keeping his eye on Eric. But he wanted to make sure that he didn't lose track of the two that were left. He wanted to make sure that he knew exactly where Phil and Mel were so that nothing could go wrong.

But by the time he found his way back to the school parking lot, classes had already started. And Lenny hadn't seen either one of them. And while he was sure that he spotted both their cars, he wasn't about to take any chances. After all, Eric's car was in the school parking lot, too. But Eric was in the basement of 333 East Harington Street. No, seeing the cars wasn't any assurance at all. So Lenny had to wait.

Until the watch went off. And he realized what a mistake he was making. And even though Lenny got lucky, even though it was only two o'clock when he woke up, he knew that if he waited around for another hour he was running the risk of dozing off again. So Lenny Seager did the smart thing, and headed for the woods.

He pushed the buttons on the watch to set the alarm, hoping that it would go off at five o'clock, the way he wanted it to. Yeah, at five o'clock Lenny would head back to 333 East Harington Street. Because from there, Lenny had figured out how to get to the video store, where Jimmy worked. And as long as Jimmy was at work, Lenny was sure that at least Mel wouldn't be going anywhere. And Mcl was the most important one of all.

Lenny closed his eyes. And as he drifted off to sleep, clutching little Bobby's ball, he thought about Mel, and how much little Bobby wanted her. Yeah, as soon as he got Mel, Lenny was sure that everything would be all better.

21

Mel couldn't shake the feeling that something was very, very wrong, that somehow the past was coming back to haunt them.

In a short period of time, three people had disappeared, without a word, without a trace. And Mel was finding it harder and harder to believe that they simply had run away. But that was what Stacey's parents believed, and Eric's parents, and the police. The note they found in Eric's car, the note from Stacey, seemed to confirm it.

Mel hadn't seen the note. The police found it when they went out to look at the car after Eric's parents reported him missing. And the note seemed to explain it all. Eric met Stacey as she'd asked him to, and the two of them had run away together. It was as simple as that. For everybody but Mel.

There were too many other questions. Obvious

questions. And she couldn't imagine why anybody else wasn't asking them. First of all, why would Stacey ask Eric to meet her in the middle of the night out on Willow Road? Mel couldn't believe for one minute that Stacey would go out behind those woods alone that late at night. And, secondly, why, if Eric did in fact meet Stacey on Willow Road, was his car in the school parking lot? And where could they have gone if neither one of them had a car?

But most troublesome of all were the baseballs. And the name Ted Williams. The nightmare that she had tried to keep buried for ten years was wriggling and squirming inside her, fighting its way to the surface. The night after Eric disappeared, Mel was startled awake by the sound of her own screams. The dream was vivid and real. She was in the woods again, just seven years old. Only this time, it wasn't Bobby Crawford who was holding the baseball, it was Eric. And out of nowhere, the monster appeared, the same man who had taken Bobby Crawford. He grabbed Eric the same way. And Mel started screaming and screaming. And finally woke herself up. And as she sat up in bed, drenched in perspiration, trying to catch her breath, she realized that the last image she was left with from the dream was that the kidnapper didn't just have Eric. Clutched tight in his other arm, was Stacey.

What if he was back? He told her that he would be. She could still see him, holding onto Bobby Crawford, who was kicking and screaming, leering at her. And he'd said in a menacing voice, "I'll be back for you." It had taken Mel years to stop believing that, years to stop being afraid, to recognize it for what it was, a hollow threat. Only now she wasn't so sure. Maybe he was back for her. Maybe he was back for them all.

Mel knew that she had to do something. But what? She couldn't very well go to the police with her suspicions. The dreams of a teenage girl hardly were cause to conduct an all-out manhunt. She had to have some concrete proof that he was back. He'd left evidence the last time, so it was only logical to assume that if he were around, there might be evidence this time, too. And Mel knew exactly where to look. Stacey had disappeared from her house, on one side of the woods. And Eric probably had disappeared from Willow Road, on the other side. There was no question in Mel's mind, if the kidnapper was back, he'd been in those woods.

And so Mel decided that she would go into the woods, back to the spot where she last saw Bobby Crawford. She wanted Phil to go with her, and Jimmy too. There was safety in numbers.

"I can't believe we're doing this," Phil said as he stepped out of Jimmy's car at the end of Willow Road. "We're not going to find anything, you know." Phil sounded as though he were trying to convince himself of that fact. He'd wanted all along to doubt Mel's suspicions, but he couldn't. To someone who'd been there ten years ago, Mel's argument had its merits.

"I know it seems crazy." Even Mel was still trying to downplay it. "But just humor me," she said.

"That's what we're doing." Jimmy tried to reinforce the tone.

And they all stood there for a minute, just looking into the woods.

"Well," Jimmy said, breaking the silence. "Shall we go have a look?"

Phil nodded, gestured for Mel to lead the way, let Jimmy follow her, and fell in behind them. It was a straight line from Willow Road to the Pattersons' back yard. And there was a path, of sorts, to follow. They wouldn't begin to see the house until they were about halfway there, almost to the spot where Mel had last seen Bobby Crawford.

When Mel took the first step into the woods she felt as though she had fallen through the looking glass. It was as though she were in a different time and place, a strange world where anything could happen, where no one was safe. She could hear the echoes of her own screams, and Bobby Crawford's, and she had to fight the urge to turn and run back out. She did turn, and saw that Jimmy and Phil were right behind her, encouraging her onward. And she knew that they were there to show her that her fears were unfounded, like parents proving to a child that there is no nightmare in the closet, no monster under the bed.

And like a child, Mel was reluctant to believe it. She approached the place with trepidation, expecting the monster to jump out and get her.

"Look at that," Jimmy said, unintentionally startling both Phil and Mel.

Mel put a hand to her mouth to stop the scream, and turned to run.

But Jimmy caught her in his arms. "I'm sorry," he calmed her. "I didn't mean to frighten you."

"You did," she scolded.

''It's okay,'' Phil assured her, having caught sight of what Jimmy wanted to point out to them. ''Look.'' Phil pointed up into the branches of a tree a short distance ahead of them.

It was a robin, perched on the edge of her nest, feeding four little chicks. Mel couldn't help but smile at the sight. ''Isn't that beautiful,'' she sighed, forgetting for a moment where she was.

''It's a beautiful place,'' Jimmy pointed out. ''There's nothing to be afraid of.''

Not for him, she thought. But she didn't say it. Instead, she forced a smile. She appreciated his efforts to comfort her. But Mel could not appreciate the beauty of the place. And she did not wish to linger a moment longer than she had to. So she began moving forward again. ''Come on.'' She beckoned Jimmy and Phil to follow. ''We're almost there.'' She glanced over her shoulder and saw Jimmy and Phil exchange worried looks.

There was nothing to mark the spot, nothing to distinguish it from any other spot in any other woods. But Mel shuddered when she reached it. It was like visiting a grave.

She looked at Phil and saw sadness in his eyes. He nodded, acknowledging that it indeed was the right place. Phil knew the spot as well as Mel. Because when the police asked her to take them there, she'd refused to go. Only Phil could convince her to go back into those woods, and only if he went with her and held her hand. Together they had led the police to the spot, both from the Pattersons' yard and from Willow Road. And even after ten years, both of them could have done it blindfolded.

''Are you okay, Mellen?'' Phil asked, using the

nickname he'd called her when they were children. It was exactly the same question he'd asked her ten years before, when she'd felt more safe with Phil than she had with the police officers.

And, just as she had ten years before, she nodded bravely.

"This is where it happened, huh?" said Jimmy.

"Yeah. Right here," Mel answered, her voice cracking. Her eyes were on the ground, scanning it. She knew exactly what she was looking for.

"There's nothing here," Phil said, sounding relieved.

Jimmy poked around the area and came to the same conclusion. "Nothing at all," he concurred. "What do you say we get out of here?" he said to Mel.

She started to nod, but then stopped. "No. Let's go a little further, closer to the Pattersons' yard."

"We're not going to find anything there, either," Phil said. "You've got to let go of this idea. You're only torturing yourself."

But Mel already had started walking, and Jimmy just shrugged at Phil and followed her. She hadn't gone more than twenty feet, when she stopped. Her eyes were fixed on the ground and she let out a small whimper and started backing away from what she saw.

Jimmy stepped in front of her protectively and followed her eyes to the object.

"What it is?" Phil asked.

"A beer can," Jimmy told him.

"Miller," Phil said automatically.

Jimmy took a closer look. "Yes."

"Don't touch it," Mel practically shrieked.

And Jimmy, who hadn't even reached out toward it, stepped back, startled.

"Fingerprints," Mel explained. "It was how the police got them last time."

"From a beer can?" Jimmy asked.

"Yes," Mel answered. "And a cigarette package."

Phil, who had moved further toward the Pattersons' property, surveying the ground, offered up the brand name again. "Lucky Strike," he said, staring down at the package.

Mel didn't have to see it to know it was there. The look on Phil's face told her. "Oh God," she moaned. And suddenly, she felt nauseous, dizzy, and trapped. "I've got to get out of here." She bolted past Jimmy, heading toward the Pattersons' house.

But Jimmy caught her by the arm, turned her around, and looked into her eyes reassuringly. "It's okay, Mel," he said soothingly, running his hands up and down her arms. "I'm here with you. And so is Phil. And nothing bad is going to happen."

"It already has." Mel started crying. "He is back. And he's taken Stacey. And Eric. And maybe even Wayne."

"We don't know that," Phil said evenly.

"We've got to go to the police," Mel insisted.

"And tell them what?" said Jimmy. "That we found a beer can and a cigarette package in the woods. Do you know how that sounds?"

"Crazy," Phil answered.

"But they're the same as last time." Mel was becoming increasingly agitated. "And there are probably candy wrappers too." She started foraging around almost wildly. "Just look for them."

"All right." Jimmy grabbed her and quieted her. "We'll look. Just calm down."

And the three of them moved back and forth, scanning the ground for candy wrappers.

"Mel," Jimmy called to her, bending to the ground to get a better look at something. "You'd better come look at this."

Both she and Phil moved to the spot.

Lying on the ground in front of Jimmy was an amethyst earring. It was one of the pair that the "secret admirer" left in Mel's car, one of the pair that Stacey had been wearing the last time Mel had seen her.

22

The story was long and complicated. But Detective Jack Doolan sat behind his desk, listening indulgently to every word as Mel explained her suspicions and the reasons behind them.

Phil sat beside Mel on the other side of the desk, giving her moral support and filling in bits of information when needed. But it wasn't going at all well. And Phil was glad that he and Mel had convinced Jimmy that it wasn't worth his taking time off from work to accompany them to the police station.

Phil watched as Detective Doolan ran his hand

over his face, pulling down the corners of his mouth, trying to conceal his amusement. Two other detectives, sitting at nearby desks, were equally amused and not quite as good at hiding it. Phil hadn't missed the sidelong glances, the winks, the grins. And he couldn't imagine that Mel had missed them either. Still, she was undaunted in her determination to convince Doolan that their friends hadn't simply run away from home.

But listening to the story, the just-the-facts-ma'am telling of it, Phil had to admit that if he were one of the detectives he would not have been able to take it any more seriously than they did. What made so much sense out in the woods sounded very different in the security of a police squad room. And Phil realized, with some degree of embarrassment, that to these detectives, he and Mel sounded like paranoid teenagers with over-active imaginations.

At least Doolan was more tactful than to say so straight out. "I'm sure this is very difficult for you," he said after Mel had finished. "And I know you must be very worried about your friends."

Mel nodded. She was sitting on the edge of her chair, hanging on his every word, waiting to hear exactly what kind of action the police would take.

"But I have to tell you honestly," Doolan continued somewhat apologetically. "There isn't much more that we can do to find your friends, than we are already doing."

Mel stiffened. And Phil reached out and took her hand, knowing that she was fighting back tears.

"You see," Doolan went on to explain. "From where I sit, there is no concrete evidence to suggest to me that a crime has been committed. And, believe me, that's good news."

"What about the beer can?" Mel gestured toward the can that was sitting on his desk. They had anticipated the fact that the police would be reluctant to go out to the woods to look at it. So they had carefully collected the evidence, making sure not to get their own fingerprints on anything. "And the cigarette pack?"

"You know what that tells me?" Detective Doolan pulled down the corners of his mouth again. "We've got a litterbug on our hands."

"They are the same brands as the last time, when Bobby Crawford was kidnapped." Mel refused to give up.

Doolan looked at the cigarette package. "Yeah. And they're the same brand my mother smokes."

"And his mother's been known to drink a beer now and then, too," the detective to Doolan's left joked.

Doolan shot him a look. "How many times do I have to tell you guys to lay off my mother." He brought his attention back to Phil and Mel. "He's right though. So for all I know, it could have been my mother who was out smoking and drinking in the woods."

Mel slumped back in her chair, defeated at last.

"Listen to me, sweetheart," Doolan said benevolently. "I'm sure that your friends are safe. Look at the facts. We've got a note from your girlfriend to her boyfriend, asking him to meet her. That strongly suggests that the two of them ran away together. And the other kid . . ."

"Wayne." Phil provided the name.

"What a piece of work he is," Doolan said, shaking his head in disbelief. "I love it. He runs away from home . . . to the Bahamas."

"What if they didn't run away?" Mel said desperately.

"What are you suggesting? That somebody abducted your friend Wayne and took him to the Bahamas? Because that's where he is. He bought a plane ticket. And he used it."

Phil saw the other two detectives practically crack up. And he heard one whisper to the other, "I should be so lucky to find a kidnapper who's willing to take me to the Bahamas."

Behind them, an office door opened. The man who stepped through it looked like a marine in a business suit. Phil recognized him immediately. "Officer Ken," he called to him.

The man looked at Phil quizzically, clearly not recognizing him.

"You'd probably do better with Captain Powers," Doolan corrected Phil, as the captain headed toward them. "Captain," Doolan greeted him.

"Hey, Jack. And who have we got here?" Captain Powers looked at Phil and Mel.

"Phil Richards and Mary Ellen Taylor," Doolan introduced them.

"You probably don't remember us," Phil piped up. "But ten years ago . . ."

"Of course." It dawned on Powers. He and his partner had been the first ones on the scene the day Bobby Crawford was abducted. He was the officer who took the little girl's statement, and tried to comfort her. "Mellen," he said, recalling the name

Phil kept calling her that day. "And Phil. How are you?"

"Fine, thank you," Mel said. "And you?"

"Good." He smiled. "What brings you down here?"

"Missing friends," Phil answered bluntly.

"They may have been kidnapped," Mel added.

Powers looked at Doolan for an explanation.

"The two Patterson kids, Wayne and Stacey. And Stacey's boyfriend, Eric Knight."

Powers nodded knowingly. "What makes you think they might have been kidnapped?" he said to Mel.

"Well." Mel hesitated, trying to compose her thoughts. "First there was the baseball. Somebody threw a baseball through Eric's car window. And it had the name Ted Williams written on it. Just like the ball Bobby Crawford had when he disappeared. And somebody threw a ball through Wayne's window, too, his dorm window. And the night Stacey disappeared, her dog had a baseball."

Phil cringed. The short version sounded even more irrational, even more circumstantial than the way she'd told it to Doolan.

"And that made us think that the disappearances might be connected," Mel continued. "So we decided to go into the woods and look around. And that was when we found the beer can and the cigarette pack, and Stacey's earring. The beer can and the cigarette pack are exactly the same—exactly the same," she stressed, "as the ones you found out there ten years ago. And I'll bet if you check them for fingerprints, those will be exactly the same too.'' Her eyes were fixed on the captain's, imploring his help.

And Phil knew, even before he said a word, that Powers would do something to appease her. Underneath his steely, by-the-book exterior, Captain Powers still was Officer Ken, a kind, and gentle, and decent man, who really wanted to help people. And besides that, when Mel put her mind to it, her stare could make a shark flinch.

Captain Ken Powers was no shark. ''Jackie,'' he said, turning to Doolan. ''Do me a favor. Send the can out to the lab and let's check it for prints. Okay?''

''Thank you,'' Mel said.

''I don't think we're going to find anything,'' Powers cautioned. ''But maybe we can put an old nightmare to rest.''

23

''I've got some good news for you, Marvin.'' He took off the lock and opened the door to the boiler room where he had Eric chained to the pipes. ''Looks like your little friends went to the police.''

Eric didn't answer. He didn't even look up.

''Isn't that great?''

Still no reaction.

''Come on, that should make you happy, shouldn't it? I mean, if the police know you're missing and all, they'll definitely come looking for you, right? And the minute they get here, you and little Deirdre can go home and live happily ever after."

Eric remained silent.

"Yeah, all we have to do now is wait for the police." He laughed. "Of course, the only problem with that is that you never know how long it's gonna take 'em to find you. So I probably wouldn't start packing right away. You know what I mean? 'Cause if I know the police, it's definitely gonna take 'em a little while to get here. In fact, there are kids out there who have been missing for like ten years. And the police still haven't found 'em. Is that amazing or what?"

No answer.

"I asked you a question, Marvin. When I ask you a question, you're supposed to answer it." He waited. "What's this? Your new tactic? Have you decided to drop the psychobabble and become Marvin the mute boy now?"

Eric gave him no reaction.

"You know, Marvin, I'm trying to be nice here. In fact, I've gone out of my way to try and make things comfortable for you, haven't I? And I'm even telling you about the police, so that you've got some hope and everything. But this obstinate behavior of yours is starting to get on my very last nerve." He grabbed Eric under his chin and jerked his head back so that Eric had no choice but to look at him. "And I thought we were friends."

Eric spat in his face.

"You know . . ." He shook his head as he let go of Eric and wiped the saliva from his nose. "I'm gonna have to hurt Deirdre for this,'' he said calmly. ''And that's a shame, because Deirdre is being such a good, little girl.''

''You bastard!'' Eric struggled to free himself from the chains.

''Yeah, Marvin, those are the new rules.'' He reached into his pocket and pulled out a candy bar. ''You be mean to me, I be mean to Deirdre.'' He unwrapped the candy and took a bite.

Eric got the message. ''Look, I'm sorry. Okay?''

He took another bite. ''Yeah? Well you don't sound real sorry.''

''I am.'' Eric's tone changed immediately. ''Honest.''

Bingo. He'd finally found the way to break Eric's spirit. ''If you're sorry, you'll tell me what your name is.''

Eric hesitated for only a moment. ''Marvin. Okay? My name is Marvin,'' he answered, defeated.

''Okay. Deirdre lives.'' He took another bite of the candy. ''Yeah, maybe I'll even keep Deirdre around until the police show up.'' He cracked up as he slammed the boiler-room door in Eric's face. ''Deirdre thinks I'm wrong, you know. About the police.'' He put the lock back on the door. ''Yeah, Deirdre seems to think that I should be shaking in my boots.'' He pulled on the lock to make sure it was secure. ''I love Deirdre; she's always so worried about me.'' He tugged on the door. ''So what do you think? Huh, Marvin? Think she's right? Think I should be shaking in my boots?'' He popped the last piece of candy into his mouth. ''Not!''

No, he wasn't worried at all. In fact, he knew it was coming. So he took care of the police the very first day he started. Yeah, even if the police were going to get involved, they were going to spend a whole lot of time chasing their tails. Because nobody was going to find George.

24

Just two days after Phil and Mel brought their findings to the police, Captain Powers called to ask the two of them back in to look at some pictures. A photo lineup, he'd called it.

"This is going to be very easy," Powers assured Mel as he ushered her and Phil into his office. "You'll see."

But Mel didn't think it was going to be easy at all. In fact, she didn't think she was going to be able to do it. She didn't think she was going to be able to identify the man who kidnapped Bobby Crawford.

She remembered the description she had given Captain Powers ten years ago. And she remembered the sketch that the police artist drew from her description. And she remembered being sure that it looked exactly like the kidnapper. But, for the longest time, so did any man with sandy-colored hair, who stood about five feet, ten inches, was thin but muscular, and wore blue jeans and work boots.

She could still repeat the description, but in her mind's eye, she could not conjure his face. And she was afraid that she wouldn't be able to recognize it either.

And Phil couldn't identify him, because Phil never saw his face. Mel wondered why Captain Powers had also called in Phil. Maybe it was because he'd been with her last time. And the time before. And maybe it was because Powers realized, even more than Mel did sometimes, how much she relied on Phil. It wasn't as though he had to do the talking for her. Most of the time he was lucky if he could get a word in edgewise. But his presence always gave her courage.

Powers sat behind his desk, and Phil and Mel took seats on the other side. "Nervous?" the captain said to Mel.

"A little," she answered, knowing that it was written all over her face.

"Don't be. You're just going to look at a couple of pictures for me. That's all." And then Powers produced them, a stack of maybe a dozen three by five photographs. He slid them across his desk toward Mel. "I want you to take your time. And look at all of them carefully. You have to be absolutely sure about anything you tell me. And if you don't recognize any of those men, that's okay too." Having given his instructions, Powers sat back in his chair to wait patiently for her to carry them out.

Mel took the stack of photographs off the desk and looked at the first one. It was black and white, a mug shot. The man had what looked to be sandy-colored hair, was not too tall, and was thin but muscular. It could have been the kidnapper. But it wasn't. Mel was absolutely certain of that. She had never laid eyes on the man in the picture before in her life. And from the looks of him, never wanted to.

She flipped to the next shot. And for a moment she thought it was the same man as in the first. She even looked at the first one again, just to be sure. And when she held the two pictures side by side she could see that they were two different people, not really so alike as she'd first imagined, but still very similar.

This was just like a multiple choice test, where all the answers could be right, but only one is. Mel wondered if she would find the right answer, and at the same time, hoped that she wouldn't.

Number two was wrong too. And she only had to glance at number three to know he wasn't the one either. Well, at least she knew who the kidnapper wasn't. Not four or five. Or six. Or seven.

Mel was just beginning to relax when she saw his face and froze in absolute terror.

Phil saw the change and moved toward her, about to say something, but Powers stopped him with a small gesture of his hand.

"This is him," Mel said in a voice barely above a whisper, without taking her eyes off the picture. "This is the man who kidnapped Bobby Crawford."

"Are you sure?" Powers asked calmly.

"Positive," Mel answered.

"Is that the man whose fingerprints were on the beer can?" Phil said.

"Yes," Powers answered. "It is."

"And on the first beer can too?" Phil wanted to know.

"Could be. But we haven't got a match yet."

"I don't understand," Phil said. "If there were fingerprints the first time, why couldn't the computers match them with this guy then?"

"Because he had never been arrested and fingerprinted until six years ago. Before then his fingerprints weren't on record," Powers explained.

Mel couldn't stand to look at his face anymore. She put the pictures down on the desk and looked over at Phil. "He's back," she told him, tears welling up in her eyes. She wished that Phil could tell her that she was wrong, that she was imagining things. But he couldn't, because now there was proof. The beer can. And the cigarettc pack. And the earring. She was thinking about the earring when Powers asked his next question.

"Have you seen this man recently?"

"No," she answered automatically. Then she thought about the earring again. And the "secret admirer." And the man in the beat-up, old car who was watching her in the mall parking lot. "Yes," she changed her answer. She tried to picture that man again. "Maybe," she said.

Both Powers and Phil waited for her to elaborate, or at least decide.

"I don't know for sure. I have seen a man who looks a lot like the one in the picture. Only he's older. And his hair is shorter. And he's heavier. But it could be the same guy."

"Where have you seen him?" Powers asked.

"Once in the mall parking lot. Somebody left

me a present. A pair of expensive earrings. With a note that said, 'From your secret admirer.' And he was parked a few lanes away, directly in front of me and facing me. And he was staring at me. And the next time I saw him was the night Stacey disappeared. He was speeding down the street, right in front of her house."

"And you're sure this is the guy?" Powers picked up the picture and showed it to Mel one more time.

"I'm sure he's the one who kidnapped Bobby Crawford. And I'm pretty sure he's the guy I saw at the mall and in front of Stacey's house."

Powers picked up the phone and punched some numbers. "I'm going to ask Detective Doolan to come in here, and I want you to tell him everything that you've just told me." Into the receiver he said, "Jack, you wanna come into my office? We've got a positive ID on George Seager."

So that was it. Finally, after all these years, the kidnapper had a name. George Seager.

25

Mel's parents had insisted that she go out to dinner with them. With all that was happening, they really didn't want her staying home alone. Under any other circumstances, Mel would have been glad to go. Only this was a business dinner, one her father just couldn't get out of. And while her parents had assured her that it wouldn't be all that terrible, she was pretty sure that it would be. Especially with the way she was feeling.

Mel was dressed and headed out the door when she realized that she just wasn't up to it. There was no way in the world she could sit at a dinner table full of adults and make polite conversation. But she didn't want to ruin her parents' evening either. So at the last minute, she asked them to drop her off at Phil's house. And, reluctantly, they'd agreed, knowing that she'd be safe, and much more comfortable.

Only Mel hadn't eaten, and she was famished. And while she was a little overdressed for the diner that was their usual hangout, she convinced Phil to take her there anyway. The idea of a cheeseburger and french fries was very appealing, so much better than fancy restaurant food that always seemed to be served in portions so small they wouldn't satisfy a dollhouse family.

They were just about to leave Phil's house when the phone call came. It was a brief conversation, and Mel only heard Phil's side of it. He didn't say much besides "uh-huh," but Mel could tell by the look on his face that it was serious. He ended the conversation with, "Okay, tell Captain Powers I'm on my way."

"On your way where?" Mel asked before Phil even had a chance to hang up the phone. The mention of Powers's name unnerved her. *Was it good news? Or bad?* "What's going on?"

"The police are out on Willow Road. They've found something that they think might be important. And they want me to come down there and have a look."

"At what?" Mel asked impatiently. She couldn't tell from Phil's demeanor if he didn't know or if he was keeping something from her to protect her. "What did they find?"

"I don't know. All the detective said was that they'd found something. And that Captain Powers asked that I come down there as soon as possible."

"So let's go." Mel headed for the door.

"I don't know if you should come." Phil sounded nervous. "I mean the detective didn't say anything about that."

"Why didn't you ask?"

"I didn't think about it," Phil answered. "Besides, I could barely make out what he was saying. It was a terrible connection. Lots of static. It sounded like he was talking over a police radio."

"Well, if they called you, they probably tried to call me, too. Just like Captain Powers called both of us the last time." She could see that Phil still was worried about her going. Worried about what might be out there that they wanted him to see. And she was worried about it, too. But if it was something awful, she didn't want Phil to have to face it alone. "I'm going with you," Mel said. It wasn't open to discussion. She moved for the door, knowing that Phil would follow. And he did.

"Who did you talk to?" she asked. "Detective Doolan?"

"No," he answered, following her outside. "It was somebody else. He said his name was Detective Ernest Johnson."

26

The end of Willow Road was dark and deserted. There were no police cars anywhere to be seen. Or any other cars for that matter. Still, Phil went all the way to the end.

"I don't get it," he said, putting the car into park. He didn't cut the engine though. And he certainly wasn't about to turn off the headlights.

"Maybe they went into the woods from the other side," Mel suggested. "From the Pattersons' backyard."

"No. I don't think so. The detective said Willow Road."

"Maybe you misunderstood. You said it was a really bad connection."

Phil considered it. It had been a bad connection. But he was absolutely certain that he was told that Captain Powers wanted him to come out to the end of Willow Road, that Powers already was out there with his officers. But as Phil looked around, there was no sign that anybody had been there. And Phil began to get suspicious. And worried. *Or maybe,* he thought to himself, *the person who called wasn't a detective at all.*

"What should we do?" Mel was beginning to sound a little worried.

"Let's take a ride past the Pattersons' house, and see if the police are out there." Phil used Mel's suggestion as an excuse to get out of there without alarming her.

He put the car in gear and was halfway through the U-turn when they saw headlights approaching. Phil sped backward, bringing his rear bumper dangerously close to a tree. But he wanted to make sure he was well on his way out of there before the other car reached them.

"Maybe that's Captain Powers now," Mel said hopefully. But the slight tremor in her voice told Phil that she was as fearful of the situation and as nervous about it as he was.

"I hope so," Phil answered her, trying to sound more confident than he felt. He put the car into drive and headed away from the dead end, controlling the urge to floor it. "You watch and see who it is in the other car as we pass him." *If he'll let us pass,* was what Phil thought but didn't say out loud.

Phil silently berated himself. How stupid could he have been? Willow Road probably was where Eric was abducted, lured there by a note that looked like it was from Stacey. And now Phil may have walked into the very same trap. And brought Mel with him.

Now, he had to get her out of there safely. He increased his speed gradually, naturally and stayed far to the right as the other car closed in on them fast. And for a moment, it looked as though the other car was moving onto Phil's side of the road, as if to force a head-on collision. Phil pulled his foot off the gas, and was ready to hit the break.

"It's Jimmy," Mel said, just as the other car moved back into its own lane. "Stop the car."

And Phil did, as did Jimmy. With the cars side by side, halfway down Willow Road, both drivers rolled down their windows.

"Jimmy, what are you doing here?" Phil was the first to talk.

"I got a phone call a few minutes ago," Jimmy explained. "From a detective asking me to come down here."

"Us too," Mel called across Phil to Jimmy.

"Yeah, well something's not right," Phil told Jimmy. He was relieved that Jimmy was there. "There are no policemen down there." He gestured toward the end of the road. "There's nobody down there at all."

"You're kidding," Jimmy said, curiously.

Phil shook his head. "Weird, isn't it?"

"You think somebody's playing games with us?" Jimmy looked up and down the street warily.

"Could be," Phil answered.

"What do you say we go somewhere else and talk," Jimmy suggested.

"Good idea," Phil agreed. "How about the diner?"

"I thought we were going to ride by the Pattersons' house to see if the police were there," Mel reminded Phil.

Jimmy's look told Phil it was a stupid idea. But Phil knew that already. "Couldn't hurt." Phil shrugged, hoping that Jimmy would acquiesce just to humor Mel.

"Fine," Jimmy said. "But if there's nobody out there, just head over to the diner. Okay?"

Phil nodded. "Do you want Mel to go with you," he offered.

"No. I don't want her getting out of the car out here. Let's just get out of here." And with that Jimmy pulled past them.

Phil waited until Jimmy had turned around and was right behind him before heading off, feeling as though they had somehow narrowly escaped danger.

Lenny Seager sat in his car, which was parked on Magnolia Lane, not a hundred feet from where it intersected Willow Road. He watched both cars pass, and waited to the count of ten before starting his own engine to follow.

27

"What the hell is going on?" Jimmy slammed the car door shut and headed around the front of the Mustang to Phil and Mel who were standing next to Phil's car just a few spaces away.

"I wish I knew," Phil answered.

"Yeah, well that makes two of us." Jimmy put his arm around Mel. "What are you doing here anyway? I thought you were going out to dinner with your parents."

"I changed my mind," Mel answered.

"Look at you, you're shaking. Are you okay?" Jimmy said, holding her.

"I'm just cold," Mel lied. "That's all."

Jimmy took off his jacket and wrapped it around Mel's shoulders.

"I just don't get it," Phil said as he looked at his watch. "We were out on Willow Road less than fifteen minutes after that detective called, weren't we?" He looked to Mel for affirmation.

Mel nodded.

"Me, too." Jimmy looked at his own watch. "I left the video store just a few minutes after I got the call."

"From Detective Johnson, right?" Phil asked.

"Yeah. Detective Ernest Johnson," Jimmy answered. "At least that's what I think he said. I could barely hear the guy because there was all kinds of static on the line."

"And what exactly did he say?" Phil continued.

"He said he wanted me to come out to Willow Road."

"For what?" Phil pressed.

"I don't know." Jimmy shrugged. "Something about Captain Powers and the investigation."

"Did he say what investigation?" Phil wanted to know. "I mean, did he mention Stacey or Eric?"

"Or Bobby Crawford?" Mel added, still shivering.

Jimmy pulled Mel in closer to him, wrapping his arms around her, trying to warm her. "No, baby," he answered, brushing the hair away from Mel's eyes. "He didn't say anything about Bobby Crawford."

Phil had never heard Jimmy call Mel "baby"

before. And it hit him like a ton of bricks. He had to look away from the two of them for a second. Because for the first time, Phil couldn't help feeling incredibly jealous of Jimmy.

"And what about Stacey? Or Eric?" Mel said to Jimmy. "Did he say anything about them?"

"No," Jimmy answered, letting go of Mel. "He didn't say anything about anybody."

"It just doesn't make any sense." Phil looked at Mel. "Why would Captain Powers want to talk to Jimmy in the first place? I mean, Jimmy barely even knows Eric and Stacey. And he certainly doesn't have anything to do with Bobby Crawford."

"Who knows," Jimmy answered him. "Maybe it had something to do with the earring and the other stuff we found out in the woods."

"Yeah, maybe." But Phil didn't remember mentioning Jimmy's name to Powers at all. Or to Doolan. And he was pretty sure that Mel hadn't either. But before he could even ask her, Mel went off in the direction Phil had been trying very hard to avoid.

"Yeah. Or maybe there is no Detective Johnson." Mel looked directly at Phil, her eyes betraying the ten-year-old fear that Phil had spent an entire childhood trying to help her forget.

And for a moment, Phil wished that Jimmy weren't there. So that he could take Mel in his arms, the way he wanted to. And tell her that everything would be okay. And that no matter what, he would never let anything happen to her. Ever.

"You know, Phil." The sound of Jimmy's voice pulled Phil's gaze away from Mel. "She's probably right.'' Jimmy's tone had an edge of anger to it. ''And I should probably kill you for bringing her out there.''

''Jimmy,'' Mel admonished, taken aback.

Phil was pretty disconcerted himself.

''Where was your head for christsake,'' Jimmy berated Phil. ''I mean, what the hell were you thinking? What are you, a moron or something?''

''Jimmy.'' Mel was furious. ''Stop it! What's the matter with you?''

''It's okay, Mel.'' Phil tried to diffuse the situation. ''Jimmy's right. I wasn't thinking.''

''No, Phil. It's not okay.'' Mel turned her attention back to Jimmy who still was glaring at Phil. ''I made him bring me. Okay? And if Phil's a moron, then you're an even bigger one, because you went out there all by yourself.''

Phil had never heard Mel talk to Jimmy that way. Ever. And while he felt a little bad for Jimmy, knowing that Jimmy was just reacting out of concern for Mel, he had to admit that he was happy that Mel had jumped to his defense. Yeah, boyfriend or not, Mel made it perfectly clear that it was a mistake to try and get between them. And that felt real good.

''Besides,'' Mel continued rebuking Jimmy, ''Captain Powers supposedly made that detective call. Remember? So how was Phil supposed to know that the police weren't going to be out there? You didn't.''

Jimmy's demeanor changed instantly. ''I'm sorry.'' He shrugged, somewhat embarrassed. ''I really am. Mel's right. I had no reason to go off on you like that.''

"It's okay." Phil meant it. "If I were you, I'd probably do the same thing." Phil winked at Mel the way he always did when he wanted to let her know that everything was okay.

"I just can't stand the thought of anything ever happening to her, you know?" Jimmy said to Phil.

"Yeah, I know." And Phil did. Because Phil felt the very same way about Mel.

"Just don't be a jerk." Mel forgave Jimmy. "Okay?"

"Okay." Jimmy smiled. Then he turned his attention to Phil. "So now what?"

"Now we find out whether or not Detective Ernest Johnson really exists," Phil answered, digging through his pockets to find a quarter. "Come on." Phil headed toward the diner as it started to drizzle. "There's a phone inside."

28

"Detective Doolan," the voice said over the line.

Phil couldn't believe it. Of all the cops on the force, Detective Jack Doolan had to be the one to answer the phone. And for a moment, Phil thought about just hanging up. Only his fear of being embarrassed was a whole lot less than his desire to find out what was going on. "Detective Johnson, please,'' Phil said into the receiver, trying to sound like anybody but himself.

''I'm sorry, Detective who?''

''Ernest Johnson,'' Phil repeated.

''I think you've got the wrong department,'' Doolan informed him.

''Are you sure?''

''Let me put it to you this way,'' Doolan said. ''I've been with this force for fifteen years, and I've never heard of a Detective Ernest Johnson.''

Phil was silent.

''Are you sure you're not looking for the State Police?'' Doolan tried to be helpful. ''I can give you that number.''

''No,'' Phil answered. ''What about Captain Powers? May I speak with him, please?''

''Sorry, Captain Powers isn't in at the moment. Is there something I can help you with?''

Phil hesitated for a second. ''Can you tell me whether or not there was a police investigation out on Willow Road tonight?''

''Can you tell me to whom I am speaking?'' The tone of Doolan's voice changed immediately and it commanded a response.

''Phil Richards,'' Phil blurted out. ''I was in before with Mary Ellen Taylor. About the kidnappings.''

''You mean the kidnapping,'' Doolan corrected him. ''Listen, kid, as far as this department is concerned, there's only been one. And that was ten years ago. Okay?''

''Yeah,'' Phil answered. ''Okay.''

''Now, what's this about a police investigation on Willow Road?''

‘‘Well . . . somebody called my house at about nine o’clock, saying that Captain Powers wanted me to come out to Willow Road ’cause there was some kind of investigation going on and he needed my help.’’

‘‘And this somebody identified himself as Detective Ernest Johnson, is that right?’’

‘‘Yes, he did,’’ Phil answered.

‘‘At nine o’clock.’’

‘‘Just about,’’ Phil confirmed.

‘‘It’s ten o’clock now,’’ Doolan pointed out. ‘‘How come you didn’t call an hour ago?’’

Phil was quiet.

‘‘Please don’t tell me you went out there,’’ Doolan continued. ‘‘Please don’t tell me that you would respond to a call like that without even bothering to check it out.’’

‘‘It sounded legit, you know?’’ Phil tried to rationalize his stupidity. ‘‘I mean, it even sounded like the guy was on a police radio or something, ’cause there was lots of static on the line.’’

‘‘Yeah? Well I’m gonna let you in on a little secret, kid. You can’t make phone calls from a police radio,’’ Doolan shot back. ‘‘So what happened when you got out there?’’

‘‘Nothing,’’ Phil answered. ‘‘I mean, the road was deserted. There weren’t any squad cars or anything. So we decided the best thing to do was get out of there.’’

‘‘No. The best thing you could have done was to not go out there in the first place,’’ Doolan admonished. ‘‘And who is this ‘we’ you’re talking about?’’

"Mary Ellen Taylor. She was at my house when I got the call."

"So this Ernest Johnson only called you?"

"No. He called Jimmy too," Phil corrected.

"Jimmy? Who's Jimmy?"

"Mel's—Mary Ellen's—boyfriend," Phil answered. "Jimmy Baxter."

"But Mel's boyfriend Jimmy didn't go with you. Is that right?"

"No. He went by himself."

"Do me a favor, kid. Back up a little."

"Apparently, Jimmy got the same phone call at work from this guy Detective Johnson. But Mel and I didn't know it until we saw him out on Willow Road. He was coming down the street, just as we were leaving."

"And you didn't see anybody else? No other cars? Nothing?"

"Nothing," Phil answered. "But we didn't stay real long. And we didn't get out of the car or anything."

"Listen to me, kid. I don't know who made that call, but there is no Detective Johnson in this department. And Captain Powers has been out of town all day. Had you called an hour ago, the way you should have done, you would have known all that."

Phil hesitated for a moment before he asked the question he was sure would have Doolan thoroughly amused. "Mel seems to think that it might have been the kidnapper, you know, that guy George Seager, who called." Phil hated saying it, but he had to. And before Doolan even answered, Phil was picturing the grin on his face.

''Uh-huh.'' Doolan's tone sounded as amused as Phil thought it was going to be. ''And is Mel the only one who thinks that?''

''I don't know.'' Phil cringed at having to answer.

''Look, kid, chances are that it was just one of your friends screwing around. That's all. Maybe even your pal Eric Knight, for all we know. And while what you did was pretty stupid, I sincerely doubt that it was anything more than a prank. However, if you should get another call from this 'Detective Johnson,' or anybody else for that matter, call me before you decide to go out and play junior G-man again. Okay?''

''Okay,'' Phil answered, feeling pretty embarrassed.

''Where are you now?'' Doolan asked.

''At Hill's Diner.''

''With your friends?''

''Yeah,'' Phil answered.

''And what are you going to do after you leave the diner?''

''I guess we're just going to go home,'' Phil said, a little confused at the line of questioning.

''Don't guess, kid,'' Doolan shot back. ''Just do it. I'll let Captain Powers know that you called.'' And with that, Doolan hung up.

And Phil headed into the diner.

29

"There is no Detective Ernest Johnson," Phil said as he slid into the booth across from Jimmy and Mel, who already were eating. "And Captain Powers has been out of town all day."

"Who did you talk to?" Mel wanted to know.

"Detective Doolan," Phil answered, picking up the cheeseburger Mel had ordered for him.

"So what did he say? Did you tell him what happened?" Mel said anxiously.

"He said we were idiots for going out there," Phil told them. "And he told me to stop acting like a junior G-man."

"You're kidding me?" Jimmy looked almost amused.

"No," Phil answered. "He seems to think that it was just somebody's idea of a joke."

"What about George Seager?" Jimmy pressed. "Didn't he think that it was at all possible that maybe he made the calls?"

Phil shook his head. "I'm telling you, he blew it off."

"I can't believe it," Jimmy said, putting his arm around Mel. "Are they at least looking for this Seager guy?"

"I guess," Phil answered.

"What do you mean, you guess?" Jimmy said impatiently. "Didn't you ask?"

"No," Phil answered a little defensively. "I didn't ask." He took another bite of the burger, hoping to drop the subject. He'd been humiliated enough for one night.

"I'm sure they're doing everything they can to find him," Mel said. "Captain Powers said they would."

"Oh, that makes me feel so much better." Jimmy was sarcastic. "Particularly since he was the cop who told you he was doing everything he could to find little Bobby Crawford, too. Isn't that what you told me, that it was the same cop?" Jimmy shook his head in disgust. "Well he did a real good job last time. Didn't he?"

Phil practically choked on his burger. Jimmy definitely was not helping the situation.

"That was different." Mel's voice dropped.

"Oh, really? If he couldn't find this guy ten years ago, what makes you think he's gonna find him now?"

"Look." Phil jumped in to try and dispel the fear that Jimmy was instilling in Mel. "Detective Doolan was probably right. It probably was just some sort of prank. Everyone at school knows about Eric and Stacey. And the more I think about it, the more ridiculous it seems. There's no way that a kidnapper is gonna call before he strikes."

Mel shot Phil a look that said she didn't believe that for a minute.

"Both of us?" Phil tried to make the point. "It doesn't make any sense, Mel. Look, even if you want to believe that this guy had something to do with Eric and Stacey. And even Wayne. They disappeared one at a time."

"What makes you think that Wayne has anything to do with this guy?" Jimmy said. "I understand why you're worried about Eric and Stacey. Because of the earring and the beer can. But what makes you think Wayne is connected?"

"The baseball," Mel answered. "Somebody threw a baseball through Wayne's dorm window. The police found it when they went looking for Wayne. I told you that."

"It may not have been a baseball," Phil reminded her. "We don't know that for sure."

"But the one in Eric's car was just like Bobby Crawford's?" Jimmy said.

Phil nodded, hoping that Jimmy would drop it.

"And the dog had a ball too, right?" Jimmy didn't drop it.

Mel nodded.

"Are the police at least taking that seriously?" Jimmy pressed.

"I don't know." Phil shrugged.

"The cops are totally worthless," Jimmy criticized.

"Let me up a minute." Mel nudged Jimmy. "I've got to go to the ladies' room."

Jimmy got up and let her out of the booth. "Don't be long, or I'm gonna panic, okay?" He sat back down.

"Listen, Jimmy," Phil started when Mel was out of earshot. "I don't want to overstep my bounds or anything. But Mel is pretty upset about everything that's been happening. And I think it might be better if the two of us tried to play it down a little bit. You know what I mean?''

Jimmy didn't answer.

The tension between them had been escalating all night, and Phil couldn't help but feel it. ''Look, I really do think the police will do everything they possibly can. And I think we ought to try to assure Mel of that.''

''What do you want me to do? Treat her like she's a moron?'' Jimmy's tone was overtly nasty. ''No. I'm not gonna lie to her. I'm not gonna tell her that everything's gonna be all right when we don't know that.''

''I know you're worried about all this.'' Phil tried to placate him. ''I'm just as worried. Maybe even more worried.''

''Yeah? Well you probably should be,'' Jimmy said it almost as if it were a threat. ''Because anybody with half a brain can see that what's happening here is no coincidence. Think about it. Ten years after Wayne Patterson pitches little Bobby's baseball into the woods, baseballs start popping up all over the place and people start disappearing. And we find a beer can and a cigarette pack in the woods with the kidnapper's fingerprints all over 'em. Does that sound like a coincidence to you?''

But before Phil could answer, Mel was back.

Jimmy smiled at her as he got up. ''What do you say we get out of here and go home?''

''Good idea,'' Phil agreed. ''Why don't you guys go ahead. I'll get the check.''

''No. We'll wait,'' Mel offered.

''Nah.'' Phil waved her away. ''Go ahead. I'm done anyway.'' He signaled for the waitress to bring the check. "You don't have to go back to work, do you, Jimmy?"

"No. Mark's closing up. Why?"

"Mel's parents probably aren't home yet . . ." Phil didn't have to finish the thought before Jimmy answered.

"Don't worry. I have no intention of letting her out of my sight." Jimmy reached into his pocket. "Let me give you some money to cover our share of the check."

"Don't worry about it," Phil insisted. "You can get me next time around."

"Count on it." Jimmy smiled.

"Call me when you get home," Mel said over her shoulder as Jimmy led her away from the table. "And be careful driving," she told him. "It's starting to pour out there."

Phil nodded. And as the waitress headed toward the table with the check, he watched Mel and Jimmy leave.

30

"Here you go," the waitress said as she handed Phil the bill.

"Thanks." Phil downed the last of his soda. And as he reached into his back pocket to grab his wallet, he noticed Jimmy's jacket lying on the seat where Mel had left it. He turned around instinctively to look at the door, thinking that maybe he could catch them. But it was too late. Mel and Jimmy already were long gone.

Phil opened his wallet to a couple of fives and a twenty. And while the waitress had been nice, there was no way that Phil was going to leave a five-dollar tip on a fourteen-dollar check. So he picked up Jimmy's jacket and headed for the cashier to pay the check and get change for a tip.

Four people stood ahead of Phil at the front counter. And the entire line was being held up by an enormous woman in spandex who was insisting that the stuffed meatloaf, which she apparently demolished in a couple of bites, should be taken off her bill. Under normal circumstances, Phil might have been amused. But with the way the night had gone, Phil felt as though he'd already been put through the wringer. And he just wanted to go home. Only the woman was creating such a scene that Phil was sure that he would be standing in line forever.

He reached into one of the side pockets of Jimmy's jacket to see if maybe Jimmy had a couple of singles. That way he could just leave all the money on the table and get out of there. But it was empty. And as he flipped the jacket around to check the other side, he noticed something protruding from the inside pocket.

At first, Phil thought it was Jimmy's wallet. And while he had no intention of looking through it—because somehow that seemed a whole lot different to Phil than just looking for loose change—he wanted to make sure that if it was Jimmy's wallet, he got the jacket back to him as soon as possible.

He didn't want Jimmy to be driving around without his license.

Phil reached into the pocket. But it wasn't a wallet. It was an envelope or a pamphlet or something. And as he pulled it out he couldn't help feeling a little bit guilty, knowing that whatever it was, it definitely was none of his business.

Until he saw it.

And he realized that it wasn't just an envelope or a pamphlet. It was an airline folder. And Wayne Patterson's boarding pass was stapled to the front of it.

Phil couldn't believe his eyes. But there it was, in black and white. Wayne Patterson. USAir Flight #406. Bahamas. And suddenly, Phil found himself looking toward the door again. Only this time he wasn't looking *for* Jimmy. He wanted to make sure that Jimmy was nowhere in sight.

Inside the folder, Phil could see airline tickets. And as he pulled the first one out, he could feel his adrenaline starting to pump. He looked at the ticket, or what was left of the ticket. It was only a receipt for Wayne's departing flight. The ticket obviously had been used. And for a moment, Phil felt somewhat relieved at the idea that Wayne Patterson really was in the Bahamas, and not the victim of a kidnapping. But the relief was only momentary, and the confusion overwhelming. It just didn't make any sense. Why would Jimmy Baxter have Wayne Patterson's plane ticket. Jimmy Baxter didn't even know Wayne Patterson.

Phil pulled out the second ticket. Wayne's return. It still was intact. And Phil's mind started racing a mile a minute. *How was Wayne supposed to get back from the Bahamas if Jimmy had his ticket? Was it at all possible that Jimmy really did know Wayne? And if that were the case, why had Jimmy been lying to all of them? Why would he pretend he didn't know Wayne if he really did?* Something was very wrong. Only Phil didn't start to realize how wrong until he looked at the third ticket.

Again, it was only a receipt. For a flight out of the Bahamas. Only it wasn't Wayne's. No. Typed clearly beside the word "Passenger" was the name Ernest Johnson.

Phil's heart started pounding so hard that he was sure the people around him could hear it. And Jimmy's voice echoed through his head, "Yeah, Detective Ernest Johnson. At least I think that's what he said. I could barely hear the guy 'cause there was all kinds of static on the line." Phil felt as if he were about to throw up. Jimmy Baxter knew exactly who Ernest Johnson was. He had his plane ticket for christsake.

Phil crammed the tickets back into the folder. And as he stuffed the whole thing back into Jimmy's jacket, an even more horrifying thought occurred to him. *What if Jimmy is Ernest Johnson? What if Jimmy is the one who made the call to lure Phil out to Willow Road?*

The lady at the front of the line still was arguing over her meatloaf, and Phil wanted to scream. He reached for his wallet and rushed back to the table.

The waitress who had served them was standing just a couple of booths away. "Listen," Phil told her. "I'm in a real hurry." He slapped the twenty down on the table on top of the check. "Just keep the change, okay?'' Phil didn't wait for an answer before he rushed for the door.

He had to get out of the diner and get to Mel. Whatever was going on, one thing was certain, Jimmy Baxter definitely was not the guy she thought he was.

31

''You're awfully quiet,'' Jimmy observed, not taking his eyes off the road. The rain was coming down hard, making visibility poor.

''Just thinking,'' Mel answered.

''This is all really rough on you, isn't it?'' Jimmy reached over and took her hand.

''I just can't believe that the police aren't taking this more seriously. Three people have disappeared.''

''Four,'' Jimmy corrected her.

But Mel didn't get his meaning.

''Four people have disappeared,'' Jimmy repeated.

She thought about it. Stacey. Eric. Wayne. And just as it occurred to her what he meant, he said it out loud.

''Bobby Crawford. Don't forget Bobby Crawford.''

''If I live to be a hundred years old,'' Mel said ruefully, ''I will never forget Bobby Crawford.''

Jimmy squeezed her hand, and smiled at her. "I know you won't," he said comfortingly.

"I just hope that Stacey, and Eric, and Wayne don't end up like Bobby Crawford." And even as she said it, Mel felt a twinge of guilt.

There was always guilt associated with Bobby Crawford, even though everybody, including Bobby's parents, told her she had no reason to feel guilty about what happened. They told her that there was nothing that she could have done to stop it. But they were wrong. She might have been able to stop it, if only she'd tried, if only she hadn't been so afraid of Wayne. And now, here she was wishing for Wayne to come home safely, when she had long since given up on Bobby Crawford. And she couldn't help thinking that maybe everything that was happening now was some sort of punishment for what they let happen ten years ago. She shuddered at the thought, gripping Jimmy's hand tighter.

"What's wrong?" Jimmy reacted. "You're not cold again, are you?"

"No," Mel answered. "Just a little shaken up," she admitted.

He looked at her, and furrowed his brow. Then he looked in the backseat. "Where's my jacket?"

"Oh no," Mel sighed. "I must have left it at the diner."

"Not really." He was clearly perturbed.

"I'm sorry." Mel was a little taken aback by his attitude.

"Damn it, Mel" he growled, hitting the steering wheel with both hands. "How could you have done that?"

Mel was startled by his reaction. And offended by it, too. The same way she'd been offended by the way he'd spoken to Phil earlier. This was a side of Jimmy that she hadn't seen before. And she didn't like it one bit. "It was a mistake," she answered icily. "I said I was sorry. Why don't we just go back to the diner and get the jacket."

Mel needn't have even made the suggestion. Because by the time she'd gotten the words out, Jimmy already was making the U-turn to head back. The car fishtailed on the slick road and Mel tensed, gasping involuntarily.

"I'm sorry," Jimmy said, once he got the car under control.

But Mel couldn't tell whether the apology was for his terrible attitude or his careless driving. And she said nothing in response.

"Look, I know I overreacted," Jimmy said, still sounding a little testy. "But it's been a rough night for me, too."

"Let's just forget it, okay?" Mel duplicated Jimmy's tone.

They rode the rest of the way to the diner in silence. The last thing Mel wanted to do was have her first real fight with Jimmy, when there were so many other problems to occupy her attention.

Jimmy raced into the parking lot and pulled right up to the door. He threw it into park. "Wait in the car," he told her abruptly, and started to get out.

Mel was astounded at the idea that he would leave her alone in a car in a dark parking lot. "I'm afraid to sit out here all alone," she answered the irritated look on Jimmy's face. She got out of the car, and followed him into the diner.

There were people sitting at the table they had occupied, a couple with a little boy. Jimmy approached the table, and Mel followed. "Excuse me," Jimmy said politely. "I left my jacket here just a few minutes ago. By any chance, was it still in the booth when you sat down?" He directed the question to the woman who was sitting where Mel had been.

"I'm afraid not," she answered, checking the seat next to her as if to be sure that she wasn't mistaken.

"Are you sure?" Jimmy pressed, looking under the table.

The woman nodded. "Why don't you ask up at the cash register," she suggested helpfully. "Maybe the waitress found it."

Jimmy spotted the waitress who had served them, and headed toward her without another word.

"Thank you," Mel said to the woman, trying to hide her embarrassment over Jimmy's rudeness, and moved after him.

"Did you happen to find a jacket at that table a little while ago?" Jimmy said to the waitress, indicating the table they'd just left.

"A jacket?" she repeated somewhat vacantly.

The waitress was young. And even Mel couldn't help thinking that the poor girl was a dumb-blond joke with feet.

"Yes," Jimmy answered through clenched teeth. "A jacket. You know what that is don't you?"

"Jimmy," Mel rebuked. Nobody deserved to be spoken to like that and Mel simply wouldn't abide it. And when Jimmy shot her an indignant glare, she returned it in kind.

"There was no jacket left at that table." The waitress directed her answer to Mel. "Not that I found anyway."

"How 'bout the guy that was sitting with us? Do you remember him?" Jimmy tried to improve his tone.

"Of course I remember him." The waitress smiled at Mel. "He left a huge tip. And he was pretty cute, too," she threw out as much to insult Jimmy as to compliment Phil.

"Did he maybe pick up the jacket?"

"Maybe." The waitress returned Jimmy's condescending tone. "But who knows. Why don't you go ask him, 'cause in case you haven't noticed, I'm kind of busy here." She turned and walked away.

"Let's go." Jimmy grabbed Mel's arm and headed back toward the door.

"Where?"

"To Phil's house."

And Mel decided that Phil's house was where she was going to stay until her parents got home. Because, after his behavior all evening, she really needed to get away from Jimmy.

32

Phil rushed into the police station like he had just witnessed a murder. "I have to see Detective Doolan," Phil insisted as he stormed the front desk. He was soaking wet and clearly out of breath.

The desk sergeant on duty reacted immediately to the urgency of Phil's demeanor. "Whoa, whoa, whoa. You wanna just calm down a little bit and tell me what's wrong."

Phil didn't recognize the officer and he had no desire to try and recount the whole story for him. There just wasn't time. "Please," Phil begged. "I really need to see Detective Doolan."

The desk sergeant studied Phil for a second, then leaned through the open door that led back into the offices. "Hey, Jack. Can you come out here?"

"Thanks." Phil took a deep breath. He needed to calm down and gather his thoughts so that he could convince Doolan that the situation needed immediate attention. The last thing he wanted to do was sound like an idiot again.

"What's up, Mike?" Doolan had barely stepped through the door, and he hadn't yet caught sight of Phil.

"Detective Doolan," Phil called to him. "Mary Ellen's missing." So much for being calm.

The desk sergeant looked confused.

"It's okay, Mike." Doolan nodded toward the door. "Why don't you grab a cup of coffee or something; I've got this."

"Sure, Jack." The sergeant stepped away from the desk.

"Now what's this about Mary Ellen?" Doolan was calm.

"She's missing."

"What do you mean, she's missing?" Doolan looked at the clock on the wall behind him. "Weren't you just with her forty-five minutes ago?"

Phil nodded. "Yeah. But after I called you, Mel left the diner with Jimmy . . ."

"Her boyfriend."

"Yeah. Only I don't think he's Jimmy."

"What do you mean, you don't think he's Jimmy?"

Phil already was sounding like an idiot and he knew it.

"Let me ask you a question, kid. Did he look like Jimmy?"

Phil nodded, knowing that Doolan was not taking him seriously.

"And he talked like Jimmy?"

Phil sighed.

"Then chances are . . . he's Jimmy."

"You don't understand." Phil was not about to give up. "I think Jimmy is Ernest Johnson."

"The infamous detective."

"Right." Phil nodded.

"And what, pray tell, leads you to this conclusion?" Doolan seemed amused.

"This." Phil handed Doolan the USAir folder. And as Detective Doolan looked at the boarding pass that was stapled to the front, Phil was sure that Doolan would soon be changing his tune.

"Where'd you get this?" Doolan's tune had changed.

"Jimmy had them," Phil answered. "And Jimmy supposedly doesn't even know Wayne Patterson."

Doolan pulled out the tickets.

"The first one is Wayne's," Phil said. "And so is the second one. But look at this." Phil practically pulled the ticket from Doolan's hand. "See." He pointed to the line. "Passenger name, Ernest Johnson."

Doolan remained calm. "And you got these from Jimmy?"

"No. I mean, yes."

Doolan looked at Phil quizzically.

Phil tried to clarify. "See, Mel and Jimmy left the diner before I did. And Jimmy forgot his jacket. So when I was standing in line . . . to take care of the check and get some change so that I could leave a tip . . .'cause I didn't have any singles . . . there was this lady at the front of the line complaining about her meatloaf . . . and I figured I'd be waiting there forever . . ."

Doolan held up his hand signaling for Phil to shut up. "Okay, kid. Enough. I've got the picture. You found the tickets in Jimmy's jacket when you were looking for some change. Is that it?"

"Yeah." Phil nodded.

"That's all you had to say."

"Sorry." Phil was embarrassed again.

"So where's Jimmy now?"

"I don't know. He was supposed to be taking Mel right home after they left the diner. But I went by her house before I came here. And nobody's there. Detective Doolan, you have to do something. Because I really think Mel might be in trouble."

"Because she's with Jimmy." Doolan's questions always came out sounding more like statements.

"No. Because she may not be with Jimmy." Getting through to Doolan felt like trying to run through a brick wall.

"Look, kid," Doolan said calmly. "I'm gonna talk to your friend Jimmy. Okay? Because one way or another, this kid's definitely got some explaining to do about these tickets."

"Don't you get it?" Phil was becoming more upset. "He's not my friend. I barely even know the guy. Nobody does."

"I thought you told me that Jimmy was Mary Ellen's boyfriend."

"He is. But they've only been going out for a couple of months. Jimmy's not even from around here. He supposedly was taking a year off before college so that he could work to save some money. And supposedly he's staying with an uncle or something."

"And where is that?" Doolan said, still undaunted.

"I don't know," Phil answered. "I don't even think Mel knows where Jimmy lives." Phil was beside himself. It hadn't dawned on him until now just how crazy that was in itself.

"So you don't know where Jimmy lives?"

"No," Phil answered hopelessly.

"What about work?" Doolan continued. "You got any clue?"

"Yeah. He works at Hit Picks, the video store down on Lalor Street."

"Okay. Now listen to me." Doolan's tone softened, just a little. "If I had to take a stab at it, I'd probably say that Jimmy Baxter—isn't that what you said his last name was when I spoke to you on the phone?"

Phil nodded, impressed at Doolan's memory.

"Okay. Chances are that Jimmy Baxter is probably hooked up somehow with Wayne Patterson. Maybe they even go to school together. And, given the airline tickets, and the fact that this Jimmy kid isn't from the area, there's a good possibility that this whole thing is the result of some kind of fraternity prank. Which may or may not include Wayne's sister and her boyfriend."

"But what about Ernest Johnson?" Phil wasn't buying Doolan's attempt to snow him.

"Look, if Jimmy Baxter is Ernest Johnson, I promise you I'll find out."

"And what about the kidnapper? What if this has something to do with him?"

"What are you trying to tell me now, kid? Huh? That you think Jimmy Baxter, aka Ernest Johnson, is actually a fifty-three-year-old ex-con named George Seager?"

Phil sighed, disgusted.

"Listen to me, I can guarantee you that George Seager was not involved with tonight's escapades. Okay?" Doolan seemed awfully sure about that.

"Now, as far as your friend Mary Ellen goes, we're going to have to wait at least another forty-seven hours and fifteen minutes before we can file a missing-persons report."

Phil shook his head exasperated.

"Hey." Doolan softened again. "I'm sure she's just fine. Maybe they stopped for some ice cream or went to a movie or something. Isn't that at all possible?"

Phil didn't answer.

"I'm sure if you call her in a little while, she'll be home safe and sound."

"So that's it? You're not going to do anything?"

Doolan laughed. "Kid, believe it or not, the department doesn't like to cut me a paycheck if I don't do anything. You know what I mean? I assure you, we're gonna cover all the bases. Okay?"

Phil nodded, feeling anything but okay.

"Now, I need for you to do me a favor."

Phil perked up.

"I need for you to go home. And stay there. I don't want you driving around looking for Mary Ellen. Or looking for Jimmy, or Ernest, or whatever you think his name is. And, above all, I need for you to keep your mouth shut about these plane tickets. Understand? Otherwise, I'm not going to be able to do my job the right way. And that really pisses me off."

"Fine." Phil pretended to resign himself to the detective's orders.

"If you have any problem at all, you know where to find me."

Like that was any help. "Sure." Phil forced a smile and headed for the door.

"Hey, kid," Doolan called after him.

Phil turned around.

"I know what I'm doing."

Phil doubted it. But he nodded anyway. And he walked out of the police station, with no intention of going home.

33

Mel was afraid they would both be killed. But she was more afraid to say anything at all to Jimmy. So she sat silently, gripping the sides of her seat as he took another curve at twice the speed limit, crossing the center line into the left lane. Had another car been traveling in the opposite direction, they would have collided, head-on.

But Jimmy had chosen to take the back road to Phil's house, a road that saw little traffic during the day, and almost none after dark. It was a road that cut through farmland, a road that was badly lit, and poorly maintained.

Fortunately, the rain had let up a little. But the roads still were wet and slippery. And Mel could feel the wheels slide out from under them every time Jimmy took a curve. Her right calf muscle was cramped from pumping the imaginary break.

And her jaw was sore from keeping her mouth clamped shut. And her neck was stiff from refusing to give in to the urge to turn her head and even look at Jimmy.

She was afraid of what she might say to him. But she was even more afraid of what he might say that would make her feel worse about him than she already did. At first, she'd only been hurt by his behavior, and surprised by it. But the more she thought about it, the more troublesome she found it. And, try as she might, she found that she couldn't excuse it.

It wasn't the way he'd lost his temper with her that bothered Mel so much. That, she would have been able to handle. That would have been a simple fight that would have blown over. What really disturbed her was the way he'd spoken to other people. He'd been more than rude. There was an underlying meanness in the way he'd treated Phil and the waitress. And she felt it still, in his silence.

He went over a rise with such speed, that the wheels of the car left the road for an instant. And when they touched down, the jolt made both of them hit their heads on the low roof of the car. Neither one of them noticed the motion up ahead until it was too late.

"Look out," Mel screamed, seeing the deer frozen in the headlights. She braced herself for the impact, already anticipating the horror of it.

But Jimmy pulled on the wheel hard, and instead of hitting the deer, the car spun off the road. And everything seemed to go into slow motion, as Mel watched Jimmy fight for control of the car as it spun around, and around, and around.

"It's okay. It's okay. It's okay," she repeated

like a mantra, as if saying it would make it so.

Finally, the car came to a stop, and Jimmy rested his head on the steering wheel, exhausted.

"Are you okay?" Mel reached out and touched his shoulder, grateful that he'd kept them alive. At the moment, it seemed inconsequential that it was his recklessness that put them in peril in the first place.

"Yeah," he nodded. "How about you?"

"I'm fine."

"This night has been one disaster after another," Jimmy said wearily, trying to get his bearings.

They were deep in a freshly plowed field. The front of the car was directly facing the road, which Mel guessed to be about thirty feet away.

Jimmy took his foot off the brake and stepped on the accelerator. But the car wouldn't move. He shook his head hopelessly as Mel listened to the back wheels spin.

"We're stuck." Jimmy told her what she already knew. "I'm gonna have to push while you steer."

Just as Jimmy opened the door to get out, another pair of headlights appeared on the road in front of them. And the car came to a stop.

"Oh, no." Mel panicked, recognizing the car immediately. She grabbed onto Jimmy. "We've got to get out of here." But she realized that there was no way. They were trapped.

Then the driver stepped out of the old, beat-up car, and stood, looking right into their headlights. "That's him," Mel cried, watching as the man whom she had identified as George Seager headed toward them. "That's the kidnapper."

She heard Jimmy let out his breath like a deflating balloon. And he collapsed over, burying his face in his hands. "Oh God," she heard him moan. "What the hell is Lenny doing here."

34

Phil was going to have to lie to get what he wanted. And that made him very nervous. Because Phil knew that he was not a good liar. He never had been. He just didn't have the stomach for it. It seemed so much easier to him, so much less complicated to own up to whatever it was he'd done and take the consequences, than to try to construct some elaborate alibi that invariably had to be protected by even more lies.

He blamed it on his parents, of course. Lying was the only unforgivable sin in his house. And the punishment for even one small lie was harsher than the punishment for any large transgression. So he grew up believing that honesty really was the best policy. And he still wished he'd followed that maxim the day Bobby Crawford disappeared. He always regretted allowing Wayne to lie to the police, and regretted even more, upholding the lie with his own silence. And even though he knew it wouldn't have made any difference, having told the truth would have eased his conscience.

But this was different. This time he couldn't tell

the truth. Nobody would believe him. Detective Doolan hadn't and he knew all the background. There was no time to try and explain all that to someone else and hope they took the situation more seriously than the police had. The quickest and most likely way to get what he needed was to lie. And, given the stakes, Phil was prepared to do it.

Phil walked into the video store and went right up to the counter purposefully. There was only one clerk behind the counter, a guy about Phil's age, maybe a little bit older, and he was waiting on a customer. The other clerk, a young woman, was busy reshelving returned videos. Phil thought about approaching her, thinking that she might be more sympathetic to his plight. But he decided against it. The information he wanted probably was on the computer, or at least somewhere behind the counter. It was best to deal with the clerk who was already there, rather than interrupt the other from her work.

The customer moved away from the counter and Phil took his place. He noticed that the clerk was wearing a name tag. *Mark.*

"What can I do for you?" Mark asked Phil.

"Is Jimmy Baxter working tonight?" Phil tried to sound as though he didn't already know the answer.

"No," Mark answered. "Today's his day off."

"He hasn't been in at all today?"

Mark shook his head.

That was just more proof that Phil was correct in his belief that Jimmy was Ernest Johnson. Out on Willow Road, Jimmy had said that Detective

Ernest Johnson had called him at work. But Jimmy hadn't been at work.

"You a friend of his?"

"A friend of a friend." Phil noticed that Mark regarded him suspiciously, or maybe he was just being paranoid. In any case, he laid the foundation for the lie he was about to tell, with a simple truth. "I'm a friend of Jimmy's girlfriend, Mel."

"Yeah, I know Mel." Mark was still a little wary. "Pretty girl."

Phil knew that he looked every bit as nervous as he felt. But that was okay. His nervousness would only serve to make the lie all the more believable. "Well, Mel's been in an accident and that's why I'm trying to find Jimmy. To let him know."

Mark's demeanor changed instantly. "Oh wow, that's terrible. She's not hurt bad, is she?"

"Pretty bad. She's at the hospital. I'm sure Jimmy would want to be there with her."

"He's gonna flip, man," Mark said, as he punched some buttons on the computer.

Phil hoped he was looking up Jimmy's address.

"I mean, he's crazy about that girl," Mark continued talking as he watched the computer screen. "Talks about her all the time." He found what he was looking for. "Here it is," he said, picking up the phone.

"What are you doing?" Phil panicked.

"Calling Jimmy's house so you can talk to him," Mark answered.

"Don't do that," Phil said a little too abruptly. He tried to salvage it. "It's not the kind of thing I want to tell him over the phone."

Mark put down the receiver. "Right."

"Yeah," Phil continued, relieved. "I thought I'd go over to his house and tell him in person. Maybe give him a ride to the hospital, so he doesn't have to go by himself." Phil paused, waiting for Mark to give him the address.

Mark looked at the computer screen and furrowed his brow. He pushed some buttons and shook his head confused. "That's weird."

"What?" Phil's mind raced ahead, searching for solutions to the problem that he knew faced him.

"His address isn't in here," Mark said. "I guess we're gonna have to call him."

"I'd really rather not." Phil began to worry. If Mark called Jimmy with this story, the trouble it would cause was unimaginable. "Doesn't anybody know where he lives?"

"Well," Mark said thoughtfully. "I gave him a ride home about a month ago, when his car was in the shop."

"Do you remember where he lives?"

"I didn't drive him to his house. I dropped him off at the Mickey Dee's on Market Street. He said he wanted to get something to eat and that he would walk home from there. So I guess he lives somewhere around there, for all the good that does you."

"It's better than nothing. I guess I'll take a ride out there and cruise the streets looking for his car."

"You sure you don't want to call? It'll be a lot faster."

Phil made believe he was considering it. "Nah," he answered finally. "You know what, I bet I'll be able to find his house without too much trouble. And I really would rather give him this news in person. I know if it were me, I wouldn't be able to deal with hearing it over the phone. And if I can't find the house, I'll come back, and we'll call him then."

"Let me save you some time," Mark said, scribbling something on a piece of paper. "Here. This is Jimmy's number. If you can't find his house, you don't have to come all the way back here. You can just stop at a pay phone or something."

Phil took the number. "Thanks," he said with genuine gratitude. He headed for the door, secure now that Mark would not call Jimmy himself.

"I hope Mel is all right," Mark called after him.

"Yeah, me too," Phil answered. And that wasn't a lie.

35

Lenny Seager felt as if the whole world was crashing down around him. And as he ran toward the Mustang, he cried out for the only thing in his entire life that ever really mattered.

"Bobby!" The sound of Lenny's voice tore through the night like the desperate howl of a wounded animal. "Bobby!"

There was steam billowing out from under the Mustang. And Lenny was terrified that at any moment, the car might burst into flames, the same way he'd seen the car on "Rescue 911" blow up. "Bobby!" Lenny roared.

The ground was wet and muddy. And as Lenny reached the edge of the road, he lost his footing and slid right down the embankment, into the front of Jimmy's car.

Inside the Mustang, Mel was screaming as if something terrible were happening to her. And just as Lenny pulled himself to his feet, prepared to shatter the side window and pull Mel out, the way he'd seen on TV, Jimmy stepped out of the car.

"Lenny," Jimmy shouted. "It's okay!"

"You gotta get away from the car, Bobby!" Lenny rushed Jimmy, grabbed him by the arm, and pulled so hard that Jimmy ended up being tossed like a rag doll, several feet away from the car. "Just stay away! You hear me, Bobby? Just stay away!" Lenny leaned into the car through the driver's side to see Mel cowering up against the passenger-side door, terrified. "You gotta get out of the car," Lenny bellowed as he reached in to grab her.

"Oh my God," Mel shrieked, kicking at Lenny. "Somebody help me!"

Lenny grabbed Mel by the ankle. And as he tried to pull her toward him, Jimmy grabbed him from behind. "Lenny, let her go! Just leave her alone!"

"But the car's gonna blow up, Bobby. Just like on '911.' "

"The car's not gonna blow up!" Jimmy was practically hanging off Lenny's back. "Now let her go!"

Lenny released his hold on Mel.

"Come on, Lenny." Jimmy pulled on him. "Get

away from the car. Okay? Just get away from the car."

Lenny moved back. Just like Bobby told him to do.

"Nothing bad's gonna happen, Lenny. I promise." Jimmy was out of breath, and covered with mud. "Everything's gonna be fine." Jimmy leaned into the car. "Listen to me, Mel, just stay in the car. He's not gonna hurt you."

Mel was hysterical. "Please, Jimmy. Please just get me out of here."

"We're gonna get out of here. Okay? Just give me a minute."

"No," Mel screamed. "It's not okay! That's George Seager!"

"Mel, just calm down." Jimmy reached out to touch her, but Mel pulled away, backing up against the door again.

"Oh my God. You know him, don't you?"

"Mel. Just take it easy."

"And why is he calling you Bobby?"

Lenny moved around to the passenger side of the car and tapped on the window Mel was leaning against to try and help Bobby calm her down.

Mel jumped forward, startled, falling against the gear shift.

"I'm not George," Lenny said, pressing his face against the window. "I'm Lenny."

Mel was frozen with fear.

"Tell her, Bobby," Lenny insisted. "Tell her I'm not George."

"He's not George," Jimmy told Mel, just the way Lenny wanted him to. "Okay?" Jimmy looked to Lenny for approval.

"Yeah." Lenny nodded. "See?" Again Lenny pressed his face against the window for Mel to see him. "I'm not George. I'm Lenny."

"Lenny who?" Mel directed the question to Jimmy, unable to control the terror in her voice.

Jimmy didn't answer, he just slammed the Mustang door shut and headed around the back of the car to the trunk.

Lenny followed.

"What are you doing here, Lenny? You're screwing everything up."

Lenny knew that Bobby was mad. And he hated it when Bobby was mad at him.

"Didn't I tell you to stay put?"

Lenny nodded contritely. "I tried. Honest. I tried real hard."

"Yeah? Well if you tried real hard, you wouldn't be here, would you?"

"I got scared," Lenny answered, ashamed of himself. And his eyes started to well up with tears. "I got scared you wasn't coming back."

"I left you with my entire life, Lenny." The tone of Jimmy's voice softened. "I left you with the ball, didn't I?"

Lenny reached into his jacket pocket to show Jimmy the baseball. "And I took real good care of it too. See?" He held out the genuine autographed Ted Williams ball. "Just like I said I would."

"I know you did, Lenny." Jimmy took the ball and put it back in Lenny's pocket. "I gave it to you because I trust you, Lenny. Understand?"

Lenny nodded.

"But you didn't trust me, did you?"

"Please don't be mad at me, Bobby," Lenny

pleaded. "I didn't mean to screw things up. I was following real good without anybody seeing me. But I was afraid you were hurt, and that the car was gonna blow up or something. And then I'd lose you for good." Lenny started to cry.

Jimmy took hold of Lenny and hugged him. "It's okay, Lenny." He patted Lenny's back. "I'm not mad at you. I'm just a little upset. That's all. Listen to me, Lenny." Jimmy pulled back so that he could look Lenny in the eye. "You've got to know I'd never leave you. You've got to know that by now."

Lenny nodded. "I'm sorry, Bobby."

Jimmy smiled. "It's okay, Lenny."

Lenny smiled back. "I found you all by myself, Bobby. You know that?"

"You did, didn't you?" Jimmy patted him on the arm like he was proud.

"Yeah. And it was real hard too."

"Too bad George isn't around so we could tell him, huh?"

"Yeah, too bad George isn't around."

Jimmy popped open the trunk. "Listen to me, Lenny. You're gonna have to help me now. Okay?"

"Sure, Bobby." Lenny would do anything for Bobby.

"We're gonna have to put Mel out," Jimmy said as he pulled the gym bag from the trunk. "You know, we're gonna have to make her go to sleep for a little while, 'cause you really scared her bad, Lenny. And now she's so frightened, that we're not gonna be able to talk any sense to her. You understand?"

"I didn't mean to scare her." Lenny meant it. "Why don't we just tell her that? Why don't we tell her that we just want her to come and live with us, just like you said."

"We will, Lenny. But not right now." Jimmy slammed the trunk shut, and Lenny followed him around to the passenger side door. Jimmy reached for the door, but Mel wasn't in the car. He pointed toward the road. And in the stream of the headlights, Lenny saw Mel trying to get to his car.

"For christsake, Lenny, you left the car running!" Jimmy tore after Mel but he slipped and fell in the mud.

Lenny ran past him. "I'll get her, Bobby. I'll get her for you."

Mel was within a couple of feet of Lenny's car when he grabbed her from behind.

"No!" Mel screamed.

"It's okay," Lenny assured her as he clamped his hand over her mouth to stifle her screams. "I didn't mean to scare you. Really. Ask Bobby."

"Just get her back in the car, Lenny!" Jimmy shouted. "Just get her in the car!"

Lenny picked up Mel and carried her, kicking and screaming, back to the Mustang.

Jimmy reached into the gym bag and grabbed the bottle of chloroform and a rag. "I'm not gonna hurt you, Mel," he told her. "I wouldn't hurt you for anything in the whole world."

"He wouldn't," Lenny concurred. And he held Mel securely so that Jimmy could put the rag over her face. "Bobby loves you. Huh, Bobby? Just like you love me, right?"

"Right, Lenny."

Mel screamed and shook her head violently from side to side, trying to avoid the chloroform-soaked rag. But Jimmy managed to get it over her nose and mouth and within seconds, Mel went limp in Lenny's arms.

"Put her in the car, Lenny."

Lenny did as he was told. And after he had gently placed her in the passenger seat, he stood there looking at her, and he smiled. "She's a whole lot prettier than we even thought she was gonna be. Huh, Bobby?"

"Yeah, Lenny. She's real pretty." Jimmy got into the car. "We've got to get the car out now. Okay, Lenny?"

"Okay." Lenny moved around to the back to push.

As Jimmy revved the engine, Lenny practically lifted the rear end of the car and shoved it forward. It took no time at all to get the car back onto the road.

Jimmy rolled down his window. "Listen to me, Lenny. I want you to get back in your car and follow me home. Then we'll figure out what we're gonna do next."

"Yeah. Okay." Lenny was thrilled that Bobby was going to let him follow, thrilled that he didn't have to hide from Bobby anymore. "Then we'll figure out what we're gonna do next," Lenny parroted, and smiled as he headed for his own car.

The 1964 Mustang that carried Bobby Crawford away ten years ago led Lenny Seager straight back to 333 East Harington Street.

36

Detective Jack Doolan knew exactly what he was doing. And as he waited for a call back from his guy at motor vehicles, who was running a check for him on Jimmy Baxter, he pulled the file on George Seager again.

Doolan had been struggling for days to try and put the pieces together. After the lab came back with the prints, and Mary Ellen Taylor identified Seager as the guy who took Bobby Crawford, there was speculation around the department that maybe the kidnapping story wasn't so far-fetched. Maybe George Seager really was somehow involved with the disappearances of both the Patterson kids and Eric Knight.

George Seager was wanted in three different states for armed robbery, a couple of liquor stores and convenience centers. But what really was disturbing was the fact that he also was wanted for questioning in two different states in connection with the disappearances of two children. Both under the age of eight. And both abducted within a year of Bobby Crawford's disappearance.

Initially, Doolan hadn't believed that George Seager was involved in these latest disappearances. Even the existence of the beer can, and the positive

ID didn't change his mind. He would have bet money on the fact that there was no way George Seager came back to town, ten years after the fact, to kidnap a couple of teenagers who happened to have been Bobby Crawford's friends. That just didn't make any sense.

He'd debated the point with several of the other detectives, insisting that the only place the obvious ever led was in circles. And, as it turned out, Doolan was right. Because at two-thirty that afternoon, he'd received a call from the Missouri State Police informing him that George Seager had been dead for nearly four months.

But Doolan flipped through Seager's file again, looking for anything he might have missed. Because now Doolan's gut was telling him that George Seager probably was involved—at least indirectly.

It was the beer can that bothered him. Either Seager dropped that can in the woods—and that was highly doubtful—or somebody who knew Seager left it there. Somebody who wanted to cover his own tracks. And that somebody really was kidnapping Bobby Crawford's friends.

And maybe worse. Captain Powers was out of town, just as Doolan had told Phil. But what he hadn't told Phil was that Powers was out of town looking at a "John Doe". A body that had been dragged from the river. The remains of a young adult, Caucasian male. And the description pretty much guaranteed that Wayne Patterson never made it to the Bahamas.

The phone on Doolan's desk rang. He grabbed

it before it rang a second time. ''Doolan,'' he said into the receiver.

''Okay, Jackie, here's what we've got,'' the voice on the other end said.

''Shoot.''

''The kid's got a license here in the state.''

''What do you have for a home address?'' Doolan said.

''The Towers Complex. 24 Sterling Street. Apartment 4-D.''

''Terrific.'' Doolan shook his head disgusted. ''It's bogus. They tore that rattrap down six months ago. What about the car? Did you come up with a registration in the kid's name?''

''Yeah. Looks like he's driving a 1964 Mustang. Plate number MX4-628.''

Doolan wrote down the number. ''Shouldn't be too hard to spot. Did you back it up for me?''

''Do you even have to ask? Backed it up all the way to Missouri. Only one title transfer. About a year ago. Your boy got his car from the original owner. A guy named Ernest Seager.''

The pieces were all falling into place. And Doolan didn't like the picture they were making. ''Thanks,'' he said into the receiver. ''I owe you for this one.''

''So what else is new?''

Doolan hung up, grabbed his jacket, and headed out of the office. He stopped at the front desk. ''Listen Mike,'' he said to the desk sergeant. ''The minute Captain Powers gets back, tell him to radio me. It's urgent that I speak to him. Got it?''

''Sure, Jack.''

''And get in touch with the Missouri State Police. Ask for Detective Knowles.'' He waited as the desk sergeant scribbled the name. ''Tell him I need anything he's got on an Ernest Seager. Radio me when you've got it.''

Doolan rushed out of the station determined to find the 1964 Mustang and to put an end to a ten-year-old nightmare.

37

Phil cruised the streets, covering a twelve-block radius around the place where Mark said he'd left Jimmy the day he'd given him a ride home. Phil was systematic and thorough in his search to find Jimmy's house, first traveling the streets north and south, then east and west. He'd even gone down the occasional alleyway. But he hadn't spotted Jimmy's car.

Three possible reasons for that occurred to Phil. Perhaps he just hadn't yet found Jimmy's house. Or perhaps he had driven past the right house, but Jimmy wasn't home. And then there was the last and worst possibility, he'd passed the house and Jimmy was home, but his car was safely hidden away in the garage.

Fortunately, the odds were strongly against that. The neighborhood was comprised of mostly row houses or semidetached homes. Very few properties had a driveway. And Phil had only counted eight garages in the entire area he'd covered.

But the further away he got from his starting point without any luck, the more he began to wish that he'd stopped to check inside each garage he'd passed. And he began to think that he probably ought to work his way backward and do just that. But when he got to the corner, he turned outward again, unable to overcome the urge to search just one more street before heading back.

Phil was determined to find Mel if he had to drive around all night. There was a reason Jimmy hadn't brought her straight home the way he said he would. And it wasn't because they'd gone to a movie, as Doolan suggested. Something was wrong. Phil could feel it.

Jimmy Baxter wasn't who he pretended to be. And he wasn't a friend of Wayne's, involved in some elaborate fraternity prank. Phil knew that for one very simple reason. Wayne Patterson would never have constructed a prank that in any way involved Bobby Crawford's disappearance. Wayne Patterson never, ever talked about Bobby Crawford's disappearance. Because Wayne Patterson was responsible for it.

Wayne Patterson hated Bobby Crawford. And, if Phil was to be honest with himself, he had to admit that he hadn't liked Bobby either. Nobody did. Bobby Crawford simply was not a very likable child. He was the kind of kid who graduated from tearing the lights off lightening bugs, to throwing cherry bombs at cats. He was the only person whom Butkus had ever bitten. Nobody saw it happen. But nobody doubted that Butkus was only acting in self-defense. Except the Crawfords, who insisted that Butkus was a dangerous animal. Even though the bite was so minor that it hadn't even broken skin, they threatened to have the dog taken away and put to sleep. And even though that never came to fruition, and even though the Pattersons managed to smooth it over with the Crawfords, Wayne never forgave Bobby.

And Wayne found the perfect opportunity for retaliation at Stacey's seventh birthday party. Bobby Crawford had been bragging for weeks about the baseball his father kept on his desk. It was a ball that was autographed by Ted Williams, a ball that Bobby's father caught at Fenway Park when he was just Bobby's age. Wayne said he wanted to see it. He dared Bobby to sneak it out of the house to show him. And Bobby did just that, expecting Wayne to be impressed not only with the ball itself, but with Bobby's daring in removing his father's prized possession from the house.

Wayne pretended to be impressed. But only until he had the ball in his hands. Without warning, Wayne ran to the back of the yard and pitched the ball as hard as he could deep into the woods. "Boy is your dad gonna be mad when he finds out that you lost his Ted Williams baseball," Wayne taunted Bobby. "He might even be mad enough to have *you* put to sleep."

Wayne got his revenge. But Bobby was only supposed to have gotten in trouble with his father, he wasn't supposed to have gotten kidnapped. And when that happened, Wayne begged the rest of them not to tell what he'd done. Wayne told the police that it was Bobby himself who accidentally tossed the ball into the woods. And the rest of them kept his secret. They never discussed it, not even with each other.

But Jimmy knew. The realization hit Phil as he made the turn onto East Harington Street. Mel would never have told him. Nor would Wayne. Nor Stacey. Nor Eric. That left only one other person in the whole world besides Phil, who knew. Bobby Crawford.

And just as Phil began wondering what possible connection Jimmy might have to Bobby Crawford, he spotted the 1964 Mustang parked in the driveway, at the end of the block. A beat-up, old car was parked in the street in front of the house, the corner unit of a block of row homes. The porch light was on, and there was a trace of light from the front window. But shades had been drawn, and curtains pulled so Phil couldn't see anything of the inside, not even shadows. But he was sure that Jimmy was inside. And he was sure that Mel was, too.

Phil drove slowly past 333 East Harington Street, wondering what he was going to do next.

38

"Mel, wake up."

The voice seemed to be coming from a thousand miles away.

"Come on, Mel."

Someone was lifting her, pulling her forward.

"Sit up."

She could feel herself being tugged at and maneuvered, propped into an upright position. But she couldn't seem to open her eyes, couldn't seem to pull herself out of the deepest, deadest sleep of her life.

"Listen to me, Mel."

The side of her cheek started to sting as if someone were slapping it.

"You've got to wake up."

Instinctively, Mel tried to turn her head away. But moving it even a tiny little bit seemed to require more strength than she could muster. She attempted to raise her hand to her face to stop the blows, but she couldn't even manage to pick up her own arm more than a few inches before she had to let it drop. Every muscle in her body seemed totally out of her control. And every limb felt weighted down.

At first, she thought that she was dreaming. Only

now, every pained sensation seemed far too real to be imagined. And as she struggled to open her eyes, there suddenly were terrifying images flashing through her mind.

She remembered the deer . . . and the car spinning . . . and spinning . . . out of control.

Maybe she still was in the car. Maybe she really was hurt, and that was why she couldn't move. Her heart started to race.

"Jimmy," Mel moaned weakly, struggling to push the sound out of her throat, as she fought against the weight of her own eyelids. The inside of her mouth felt as though it were lined with cotton. And her tongue felt swollen and parched.

"I'm right here, Mel."

The hand stroked her hair comfortingly.

"I'm right here."

She could barely make out the face. Everything was foggy and out of focus. She clenched her eyes shut, then opened them again, hoping to clear her vision. Only everything was still blurred. But the voice was much clearer. And Mel knew that it was Jimmy's voice. She definitely was with Jimmy. Only they weren't in the car. Not anymore. Because through the haze, Mel could see the room around her reeling. "Where am I?" Her voice was barely audible.

"With me, Mel. You're with me," Jimmy answered her. Then he turned toward the enormous figure of a man seated across the room. "Go get some water."

Mel couldn't make out the figure, couldn't see him clearly. Again she closed her eyes, hoping to regain control of her perception.

"In the kitchen?"

The sound of the voice coming from the other side of the room stopped her heart. And she could feel her breathing becoming more labored and shallow.

"Yeah," Jimmy answered. "In the kitchen."

"Okay, Bobby."

It was as if the name itself started to pull Mel out of her daze and send her into a horrifying reality. And now she didn't want to open her eyes. She didn't want to have to see things clearly.

Images of the accident quickly were replaced by clouded memories of the series of events that followed. And within moments, there was no escaping the face of George Seager that was burning itself into the darkness of her mind. Panic was quickly replacing confusion. And in a knee-jerk reaction, Mel tried to get up quickly, to get away. Only it was futile. And what she thought had been an enormous leap actually had just been a small push forward. But the attempt alone created so much discomfort that Mel cried out in pain.

"It's okay, Mel. You're okay."

Mel's vision was starting to come into focus. But now the clear sight of Jimmy offered no comfort at all. And the imagined face of George Seager suddenly was replaced with the actual one.

"Here you go, Bobby."

"Thanks, Lenny." Jimmy took the glass of water.

Mel's eyes were fixed on the man standing beside Jimmy. *I'm not George,* he had said. *I'm Lenny.* The words replayed themselves in her head.

''Here, Mel. Drink this.'' Jimmy pulled her head forward.

Mel struggled to turn away.

''It's just water, Mel. Honest. It's not gonna hurt you.''

''Yeah,'' Lenny agreed. ''It's just water.''

Mel refused to part her lips as Jimmy held the glass to her mouth.

''I'm just trying to help you, Mel.'' Jimmy sounded testy. ''Now drink.'' He pressed the glass against her lips harder.

But still Mel refused.

''Fine.'' Jimmy slammed the glass down on the table in front of the couch.

''It'll make you feel better,'' Lenny said, leaning over to pick up the glass. ''Really.'' He held it out to Mel.

There was a gentleness in his voice. And Mel couldn't help but notice it, even though she was terrified by his presence. And she was more terrified by the fact that he kept calling Jimmy ''Bobby''.

''Every time George used to knock me out,'' Lenny continued. ''I'd drink lots of water when I woke up. 'Cause everything's all dry. Right?''

Lenny's eyes were warm, and soft. Not the eyes of a predator. Not the eyes that had burned themselves into her memory ten years ago.

''For christsake, Lenny.'' Jimmy grabbed the glass from him. ''I thought I told you to keep your mouth shut about George. Remember?''

''Yeah, Bobby. But I was just trying to tell her that the water'll help.'' He looked at Mel again. ''George used to practice on me all the time with the rag . . . you know . . . so that he'd get it right. And that's why I know you gotta drink a lot when you wake up." He smiled at her. Then he looked at Jimmy. "I just wanted to tell her that. That's all. That's not really about George, Bobby." He looked at Mel. "That's about me, huh?"

There was an innocence to the man. And Mel found herself wanting to answer him. Suddenly, Jimmy's presence seemed much more threatening to her than the overwhelming bulk of the man standing over her—the man who was talking about George. Mel couldn't seem to put it together. But she knew it was Jimmy who'd knocked her out, Jimmy who'd orchestrated everything. And as her mind started to clear, she remembered that the man who called himself Lenny had been insisting that the car was going to blow up. And he just wanted to get her out. He just wanted to save her life.

"Right," Mel answered him, gaining a little more control over her voice.

Lenny picked up the glass again and held it out. "See, Bobby? It's okay."

Jimmy took the glass and held it again to Mel's lips.

This time she drank.

"Well, well, well," Jimmy said sarcastically. "I didn't think the two of you would hit it off so quickly."

"Why, Bobby?" Lenny sounded upset. "I like her. I like her a lot."

Jimmy laughed. "I wasn't really worried about you, Lenny. I was worried about Mel." He stroked her hair.

And Mel went rigid against his touch.

''You amaze me, Mel,'' Jimmy sounded dejected. ''Lenny tells you to drink, and you drink. I try to help you, and you pull away. Why is that, Mel? Don't you trust me anymore?''

''Trust you?'' Mel couldn't stop the reaction. ''I don't even know you.'' She could feel tears welling up.

''Yes you do, Mel.'' Jimmy touched her cheek. ''Better than you think.''

''Come on, Bobby, let's tell her now. She's wide awake. And you said we would tell her when she woke up. So can we? Can we tell her now?''

''Yeah, Lenny. We can tell her now. Thanks to you, we don't have much of a choice.''

''Tell her about me first, okay? Tell her about me.'' Lenny was excited, like a little kid about to share a secret.

And Mel was sure that whatever explanation there was to offer about Lenny, it wouldn't be nearly as bad as whatever Jimmy had to say about himself.

''Lenny saved me, Mel,'' Jimmy began. ''He wants me to start this way.''

Lenny smiled, proud of himself.

''In fact, if it weren't for Lenny, I'd probably be dead by now. Although''—Jimmy's tone changed—''there were days when dead would have been a blessing.''

Mel listened intently as the old nightmare began to surface.

''You see, the reason that you were so afraid of Lenny, Mel, is that Lenny looks a whole lot like his brother.''

Mel anticipated his next words before he said them.

"George. Lenny's brother was George Seager. I say 'was' because George Seager is no longer with us. No, George Seager can't hurt anybody anymore. Huh, Lenny?"

"George can't hurt nobody anymore," Lenny attested.

"But you were right, Mel. George Seager was definitely the guy who took Bobby Crawford," Jimmy went on. "Took away his entire life . . . just so he could sell him." Jimmy looked at Mel, his eyes full of pain. "You'd be amazed at the kind of sick people there are in this world, Mel . . . people who are willing to pay big bucks just to get their hands on a seven-year-old little boy. But Lenny wouldn't let George sell Bobby." He smiled at Lenny. "Huh, Lenny?"

"No." Lenny shook his head. "I wasn't gonna let George sell Bobby. I told George he was just gonna have to kill me first before he sent little Bobby away."

"He almost did too," Jimmy told her. "In fact, Lenny never raised a hand to George until the day George tried to get rid of little Bobby. And that day"—Jimmy smiled as if recalling a fond memory—"Lenny beat the crap out of George."

Lenny looked proud of himself.

"And little Bobby was amazed," Jimmy continued. "Because Lenny had protected him. And from that day on, little Bobby loved Lenny with all his heart."

" 'Cause Lenny loved little Bobby, too," Lenny added, making sure he had Mel's attention.

"Yeah." Jimmy smiled at Lenny. "Lenny always loved Bobby, too."

Mel's heart was aching.

"Did I tell her right?" Jimmy asked Lenny.

"Yeah." Lenny nodded. "Now tell her about the time we got in trouble with George because I was gonna bring you back to get her."

"I need to tell her about little Bobby first, okay?"

Lenny nodded.

There was a part of Mel that just didn't want to know. It was the same part of her that for ten years had managed to suffocate even her wildest imaginings about what really happened to Bobby after the kidnapping. And for the very first time, Mel found herself wanting to believe that Bobby Crawford really was dead, the way everyone had accepted him to be.

"Next to Lenny, you were the only thing that kept little Bobby going, Mel. The only part of his real life that he could cling to. You see, once George told little Bobby that he'd murdered his parents, little Bobby had nothing left. Nothing. Except the baseball, and the hope that one day he'd be with you."

Mel couldn't handle what she was hearing. And she didn't want to believe a word of it. The idea that she could mean so much to Bobby Crawford was overwhelming, and totally out of the realm of any kind of childhood reality. If Mel were to be brutally honest with herself . . . before Bobby Crawford disappeared . . . before his memory became glorified . . . in the same way one remembers a slain president or an unknown soldier . . . her only real perception of him was that he was an obnoxious, little kid who happened to live in the same nieghborhood, and whose presence usually was unwanted. And while she never went out of her way to be mean to him, the way Wayne and some of the other kids did, she never really treated him as anything other than an acquaintance. He certainly was not counted among her close friends.

"And Lenny did try to bring little Bobby back to get you once. Because Bobby told Lenny how much he cared about you, Mel. And how much you cared about him." Jimmy paused, staring at Mel, trying to read her thoughts.

And Mel tried not to allow the expression on her face to betray what she was feeling. Because somehow, she knew that would be a mistake.

"Yeah." Jimmy finally went on. "Little Bobby told Lenny all about the way you followed him into the woods to try and help him find the ball. And how you screamed for him when George grabbed him and took him away. And Lenny cried. Didn't you, Lenny?"

Lenny looked as if he might cry again, just listening.

"But George found out. And he told Lenny that if he ever tried to do such a stupid thing again, he was gonna put him in a home. Didn't he, Lenny?"

Lenny nodded sadly. "George said he was gonna put me in the nuthouse."

"And George made little Bobby spend two months chained up in a closet." Jimmy shook his head as if to shake out the memory. "So after that, little Bobby knew that he had no other choice but to wait until he was old enough to get rid of

George, and come find you on his own.'' Jimmy smiled as he knelt down in front of her.

Mel felt as if at any moment she might throw up from all the mixed emotions that were whipping around inside her. She had been trying to hang onto the idea that Lenny Seager was just confused, and Jimmy Baxter had some other relationship to George Seager than the one she feared most. Only now that was becoming an impossible thing to do.

Jimmy reached out and took her hand. ''And now he has, Mel. Now he has,'' Jimmy whispered intimately.

''It's impossible.'' Mel was unable to silence her dismay.

''No, Mel. It really is me.'' Jimmy pulled her close and hugged her.

Mel's body went rigid.

''What's the matter, Mel? Aren't you happy that it's me? Aren't you grateful that we're together again?'' He was more angry than dejected.

Mel fought to stay cool, knowing that she might very well be fighting for much more. ''It's just . . .'' Mel struggled for something to say, something that wouldn't upset him any more than he already was. ''It's just that you don't look like Bobby. That's all. I mean, the way I remember him.'' That was the truth.

''How do you remember Bobby, Mel?'' he baited her.

''Bobby had dark hair. And brown eyes. Beautiful, dark brown eyes,'' she added in an effort to ease the tension between them.

His only response was to pop out one of the contact lenses that Mel had no idea he wore. And then the second. He looked directly into her eyes and Mel's breath caught.

"Like these?" He grinned like the Cheshire cat.

Mel nodded numbly, wanting more than anything to be able to turn away. But she didn't dare.

"See?" Lenny beamed.

And Mel was grateful for the sound of Lenny's voice because it allowed her to turn her attention to him.

"It really is Bobby," Lenny assured her.

Mel forced a smile.

"Now we can bring her home with us so that we can all live together. Huh, Bobby? Just like you said."

"Yeah, Lenny." Jimmy didn't take his eyes off Mel for a second. "Now we can take her home with us."

Mel was sure that Jimmy could read the terror in her eyes. And as her mind raced, searching for something to say that wouldn't put her in a worse position than she already was, the sound of someone banging on the front door made her jump.

"Stay quiet," Jimmy commanded. He got up and headed down the hallway to the door.

Mel strained to watch him, aware that Lenny was watching her. She saw Jimmy peek through the curtain, carefully, so that the movement would be indiscernible from the outside.

Jimmy stepped back into the room. "Phil's here," he announced as if Phil were expected company. He smiled sardonically. "How nice."

39

He opened the door to see Phil standing on the front porch, trying to look casual. And it really amused him.

"Hey, Jimmy." Phil tried to control the uneasy tone of his voice.

"Phil," he feigned surprise. "What's up?" He was much better at this game than Phil ever could hope to be. After all, little Bobby had spent ten, long years learning how to perfect the art of deception. And watching Phil squirm was a lot of fun.

"You left your jacket at the diner." Phil held it up. "And I just wanted to return it to you."

"Gee, that was really thoughtful of you." He opened the screen door and stuck his hand out.

Phil didn't move.

"I really appreciate it." He waited.

Reluctantly, Phil handed him the jacket.

He took it, then closed the screen door. And he had to stop himself from laughing at the sight of Phil, standing in front of him like an idiot, struggling to come up with another move. Yeah, maneuvering Phil into checkmate was going to be a piece of cake. "How did you know where I lived?" he said innocently, as he felt the jacket for the tickets.

And Phil squirmed. "Mel mentioned it once," he lied badly. "And I guess I just remembered it."

"Oh." He was going to leave it alone. Rule was, when you were playing this kind of game, it was always better to hand your victim enough rope to hang himself. "Well . . . thanks a lot." He stepped back as if he were going to close the door.

"Is Mel here?" Phil said, unable to conceal the urgency in his voice.

And this time he almost did crack up. Although, on a level, it probably was better that Phil was stupid enough to go straight to the point. It would save a lot of time. "Why? Should she be?"

Phil was quiet.

He watched as Phil's little brain ticked away, trying to find a good answer. What a shame that Phil wasn't going to be able to provide him with any kind of a challenge. Yeah, it was quite clear that there was just no point in prolonging the play between such mismatched rivals. "She's here," he answered. "Come on in." He opened the door, inviting Phil inside.

Phil stepped through the door into the hallway.

"By the way, Phil," he said nonchalantly as he closed the inside door and locked it. "What happened to my tickets?"

Phil froze.

"Are they in your car?" he said calmly. "Or in your pockets?" He felt Phil's pockets as if he were frisking him. "Or did you do something really stupid with them, Phil? Did you go running to your little policeman friend again?"

"I don't know what you're talking about, Jimmy."

“You did something really stupid with them, didn’t you?” He could feel the blood rushing to his head. And while he was sure that the cops had no idea who he really was, and that Phil had come alone, he knew that sooner or later they would start looking for Jimmy Baxter. So now he was going to have to make Jimmy Baxter disappear a lot quicker than he’d intended. There was no more time for playing games. “You know, Phil,” he raged, figuring that there was no reason to control his anger anymore, “you really piss me off.” He grabbed Phil by thc back of the collar and dragged him into the living room before Phil had a chance to react.

“Look, Mel.” He threw Phil into the chair next to Lenny. “Phil’s here.”

The sight of Lenny held Phil in place, just the way he knew it would.

“That’s Lenny Seager, Phil. George Seager’s brother. Make one move, and I promise you he’ll snap your neck. Won’t you, Lenny?”

It was the wrong thing to say. Lenny started to fidget nervously, the way he used to do whenever George tried to force him to do something really bad. But he knew what to say to remedy the situation. “Lenny will do whatever he has to do to protect me. Right, Lenny?”

“Right, Bobby,” Lenny answered without hesitation.

At the mention of the name Bobby, Phil’s eyes widened.

“I’m sorry. Where are my manners. I ought to reintroduce myself to you.” He grabbed Phil’s hand and shook it, hard. Painfully hard, he hoped.

"Bobby, Phil. Bobby Crawford. It's been a long time, hasn't it?" He released his grip on Phil's hand, content that he'd caused sufficient pain, both physical and emotional.

Then he saw Phil look at Mel. He saw their eyes meet, saw the concern they had for one another. There was a silent communication between them. The bond between Phil and Mel, that had existed even when they were children, charged the room.

Bobby Crawford wouldn't allow that. He stepped between them, blocking their view of one another. "So listen, Phil. I'd love to stay and shoot the breeze with you. You know, catch up on everything. But thanks to your stupidity, there really isn't any time for that now."

He moved right in front of Phil. "But I have to ask you one question." He grabbed Phil by the throat. "How did you really find this house?"

"Please, Jimmy," Mel begged. "Don't hurt him!"

He shot Mel a warning look to stay where she was. "Bobby, Mel," he corrected her harshly. "Bobby! And he deserves to be hurt." He tightened his grip. "I'll ask you one, last time," he said to Phil. "How did you find the house?"

"Mark," Phil choked out. "At the video store. He said he dropped you off in the area one time. I cruised the streets until I found your car."

One mistake. One, stupid mistake.

"Before or after your visit to your pal 'Officer Friendly?' "

"After," Phil answered. "After."

He thought about just squeezing the life out of Phil. Killing him probably would feel as good as it felt to kill George. And then Phil Richards would become nothing more than another buried memory. Bobby tightened his grip even more.

"Please, Bobby," Mel cried. "Please don't."

Bobby. Mel finally called him Bobby. He'd waited ten years to hear his name from her lips again. And just for her, just to prove his undying love, he released his hold on Phil.

Phil fell back in the chair.

And Bobby went to Mel. He knelt down in front of her and took her hand. "He doesn't deserve your compassion, Mel. You've got to know that."

Mel looked away, tears running down her face.

"Don't you remember how he laughed, Mel? Don't you remember how funny he thought it was when Wayne threw my ball into the woods? Instead of trying to stop Wayne, he laughed. So how can you feel anything for him?"

"It wasn't Phil's fault, Bobby," Mel insisted. "It wasn't anybody's fault," she sobbed.

He raised his hand to slap her, but managed to stop himself. "How can you say that, Mel?" He worked hard to control his rage. "It was everybody's fault. Wayne's. And Stacey's. And Eric's. And Phil's. It was everybody's fault but yours. And now they have to pay. Can't you understand that? It's only fair."

"No." Mel shook her head defiantly. "I don't understand."

"Stacey understands."

Mel looked at him, horrified.

"And you know what? I really believe that she's sorry too, Mel. Yeah, now that Stacey understands just what it feels like to have your entire life ripped away, she's awfully sorry about what happened at her seventh birthday party.'' He smiled. ''And Eric's coming along, too. Only now I can't stick around to watch his progress. Because now, thanks to Phil, we're gonna have to leave here, Mel.''

Bobby stood up and turned to face Phil again. ''You know, Phil, leaving you is going to be a real letdown. Almost as big a letdown as Wayne was. The only difference is that when I leave you, you'll still be breathing.''

''Wayne's dead?'' Mel gasped.

Bobby nodded. ''But it was his own fault,'' he told her.

''Listen, Bobby,'' Phil pleaded. ''I know that what happened to you wasn't fair. But what you're doing isn't going to make it any better.''

''Oh, I don't know about that.'' Bobby laughed. ''I'm feeling better and better all the time. And you know what would probably make me feel even better still. Killing you. Right here. Right now. And if it weren't for the fact that Mel would never forgive me for that, I'd probably do it, too. So, just for her sake, I'm gonna give you a fighting chance. I'm gonna chain you up like an animal . . . just like I was chained up, Phil. And I'm gonna leave you here . . . in the basement . . . with Stacey and Eric . . . who, by the way, will only answer to their new names . . . Deirdre and Marvin. Awful names, huh? But not nearly as bad as Ernest Johnson.''

''Ernest is the worst name,'' Lenny jumped in.

Bobby smiled at Lenny.

But he still had plenty of hatred left for Phil. ''Yeah, you and Stacey and Eric can all rot together. But who knows, maybe your pal 'Officer

Friendly' will find you before you dehydrate and go into convulsions and mercifully die.'' What a pleasant thought that was.

''It doesn't have to be this way, Bobby.'' Phil sounded like a psychologist.

''No, I guess it doesn't.'' Bobby paused as if he were really thinking it over. ''But it's gonna be.'' He laughed. ''Lenny, take our friend down to the basement and chain him up real good. Just like George made you do to me. And don't forget to gag him.''

''Okay, Bobby.''

Phil was smart enough not to even try to resist Lenny.

''Don't hurt Mel, Bobby,'' Phil begged as Lenny dragged him away. ''Just don't hurt Mel.''

''Phil!'' Mel scrambled to her feet. But she still was weak and it took little effort for Bobby to restrain her.

''One day you're gonna thank me for this,'' he told her.

Mel started screaming and screaming just the way she had the day George kidnapped Bobby. Only this time, the name she was calling was Phil.

Bobby clamped his hand over her mouth. ''Now you listen to me, Mel. I don't want to have to knock you out again. That could be dangerous. Because there's a good chance you won't wake up again. But if you don't calm down, you're gonna leave me no choice. Do you understand me?''

She nodded, defeated.

''Good. Now you and Lenny and I are getting out of here. I'm taking you home.''

Mel looked at him hopefully.

"My home," he clarified. "And I had really hoped that you would come with me willingly. But I guess you need some time to come around. Unfortunately, there's no way I can trust you to ride in the car with me. So I'm gonna have to put you in the trunk, Mel. But don't worry. It's not so bad. Not nearly as bad as you think. And it'll be a whole lot easier on you if you just relax. Don't fight me, Mel," he warned. "I don't want to have to hurt you. But if you force me to, I will."

40

Detective Jack Doolan spotted the 1964 Mustang in the driveway at the end of East Harington Street. There was a young man walking away from the car. He stopped to take note of Doolan's approach. And, assuming that this was his guy, Doolan pulled his car into the driveway behind the Mustang and got out.

"Jimmy Baxter," Doolan called.

He looked at Doolan. But he didn't say anything. He didn't have to. His face told Doolan everything he needed to know.

"Detective Jack Doolan," he introduced himself casually as he walked toward the porch.

Jimmy started to back off the porch, moving toward him. "What can I do for you, detective?"

The kid looked a little too anxious to please. And

he didn't want Doolan near the house either, wanted to keep him out on the sidewalk. There was trouble. "I was hoping that you could answer a couple of questions for me."

"I'll do my best," Jimmy answered affably.

"You think maybe we could talk inside?" He knew what the answer was going to be, but it was worth a shot, since he didn't have a search warrant.

"Well you see, detective," Jimmy fudged. "I live with my uncle. And tonight's his poker night. He and his buddies are inside playing cards. And it would just be, you know, a little weird if I came walking in with a cop."

Doolan nodded noncommittally, letting Jimmy wonder whether or not he believed the story. "No problem. We can talk out here. I understand that you're Mary Ellen Taylor's boyfriend."

"That's right. We've been seeing one another for a couple of months."

"And did you see her this evening?"

"Yeah, I did. I took her out earlier, to get something to eat."

Doolan heard a noise behind him. He turned toward the sound, but saw nothing. And when he turned back toward Jimmy, he noticed that Jimmy wasn't hiding his discomfort as well as he had been. "And what time was that?"

"I must have dropped her off at around ten o'clock. Maybe ten-thirty."

"Uh-huh," Doolan said, noticing that Jimmy was having trouble maintaining eye contact. His eyes kept wandering to the left of Doolan, looking past him. A quick glance in that direction told Doolan he was looking at the Mustang. "Well that's strange,'' he continued. ''Because Mary Ellen Taylor is not at home.''

''You're kidding?'' Jimmy looked duly shocked and concerned. ''How do you know that?''

''Her parents called to report her missing,'' Doolan lied, and he did it much better than Jimmy did. ''They felt silly doing it, but with three of her friends missing, they're understandably nervous.''

''I don't know what to tell you, detective.'' Jimmy did his best impression of the worried boyfriend.

''No idea where she might be, huh?''

''None,'' he answered, sounding hopeless.

''Well, don't panic yet. There are a couple of other places I need to check before anybody starts getting nervous.'' Doolan headed back toward his car, as if he intended to leave. ''If you think of anyplace she might be, give us a call, okay?''

''Sure thing.''

He stopped beside the Mustang. ''Great car,'' he said, checking it out. ''Beautiful condition.'' He looked through the windows. ''Is it yours?''

''Yeah,'' Jimmy answered.

Strange reaction from a kid who had a car like this. Anyone who owned a classic car in mint condition generally bent your ear telling you all about it. ''So how'd you end up with a car like this?''

Jimmy hesitated. ''It was my uncle's car. He gave it to me.''

''Your uncle who's playing cards inside?''

Jimmy nodded nervously.

And Doolan could see that he was losing his cool fast. And then he heard the noise again. It was coming from inside the trunk. But Doolan didn't react this time. Instead, he fixed a steely glare on Jimmy.

Jimmy's eyes darted around. And Doolan knew that he was looking to bolt.

"Don't even think about it." Doolan pulled his gun. "Now I want you to walk over here nice and slow and open this trunk for me."

"My keys are in the house."

"Then we'll go in the house and get them."

And just as Doolan took his first step toward Jimmy, the front door crashed open and a goliath of a man rushed out. "Don't you dare hurt Bobby," the man roared.

And Doolan knew in that instant that his hunch had been right. Improbable as it had been, it was Bobby Crawford who'd been abducting his old friends. But there was no time to think about that now because the man was headed toward him. "Don't move," Doolan warned the man, taking careful aim.

He didn't listen.

"Lenny," Bobby shouted. "Stop! It's okay. Just stay where you are!"

Lenny obeyed.

"Please," Bobby appealed to Doolan. "Please don't hurt him. Lenny isn't responsible for any of this. He doesn't always understand what's going on. You know what I mean?"

Doolan knew. He knew all about Lenny Seager. The desk sergeant had radioed not five minutes before with the Missouri State Police report.

Doolan saw the squad car approaching. He'd asked to have a patrol car take a ride by the house just to make sure everything was all right. He didn't think he'd need it. But he certainly was glad he asked for it.

The officers responded swiftly to the sight of Doolan with his gun drawn. Immediately they were out of the car, drawing their own weapons.

"It's okay," Doolan assured them. "Lenny," he said, looking right at him, "the officer is gonna put you in handcuffs. Please don't do anything stu—" Doolan stopped himself from using the word stupid. "Please don't try to resist him. He's not gonna hurt you. And nobody's gonna hurt Bobby, either. Okay?"

Lenny was frightened and confused, and he looked to Bobby for answers.

"Do what he says," Bobby told him.

Lenny stood perfectly still as one of the officers cuffed him and patted him down. But he became agitated when the officer reached into his pocket and pulled out the baseball. "No!" Lenny cried. "That's Bobby's ball. I have to take care of it. That's Bobby's whole life."

Doolan took a look at it. The baseball, autographed by Ted Williams. Under any other circumstances he would have gotten a real kick out of seeing a collector's item like that. But that baseball had been the cause of so much pain and suffering and loss, that Doolan couldn't appreciate the nostalgic value of it. He motioned for the officer to give it back to Lenny.

"You take care of it. Okay?" Bobby told him.

Lenny smiled. And the ball was replaced in his pocket. Then the officer led him toward the squad car.

To the other officer, Doolan said, "Take him inside and get his car keys so that we can open this trunk."

"They're in my pocket," Bobby admitted.

Bobby started to reach into his pocket for the keys, but the officer stopped him and got them himself. He tossed the keys to Doolan.

"Cuff him," Doolan ordered.

"Detective," Bobby said. "Lenny didn't do anything. He isn't responsible for anything George Seager did. And he isn't responsible for what I've done."

"I understand that," Doolan assured him. He really felt for the kid. And, as tough a cop as Doolan was, he couldn't help thinking that Bobby Crawford wasn't entirely responsible for what he'd done either. He shook his head sadly as Bobby Crawford was led to the squad car.

Doolan moved to the trunk of the Mustang and opened it. Inside, he found Mel, bound and gagged, and wrapped in a heavy blanket. The look of terror on her face nearly broke his heart.

"It's okay, sweetheart," he said gently, as he removed the gag. "You're safe now."

She started to cry with relief. "Thank God," she choked out. "Thank God." She looked Doolan right in the eye. "Thank you."

He smiled reassuringly and went to work unbinding her hands and feet. "You okay?"

"Yes." She nodded bravely.

"They didn't hurt you?"

She shook her head no.

"Well we've got them both in custody now. It's all over."

"Did you find my friends?" she asked hopefully. "They're all inside somewhere."

"Stacey and Eric?"

"And Phil," she added.

Doolan shook his head exasperated. "I can't believe Dick Tracy got here before I did," he muttered to himself.

"Huh?" Mel looked at him confused.

"Nothing," he laughed. "Nothing to worry about. You're all safe now."

He lifted her out of the trunk and she caught sight of thc squad car. But she turned her head away and started crying again. Doolan gave her a minute. He put a protective arm around her.

"Lenny Seager didn't do anything," she said finally. "He's not a bad man. He's . . ."

"I know," Doolan interrupted. "I know all about Lenny. Trust me, we're gonna do the right thing. We're gonna take care of him."

"And Bobby?"

"We're gonna make sure they both get the kind of help that they need."

Mel nodded, content with that answer.

"Come on," Doolan said. "Let's go inside and take care of your friends."

41

It was one minute to midnight. And the room was quiet, everyone eagerly anticipating the ten-second countdown. The theme of the senior prom was "The New Year." Mel had thought it was pretty corny when the class had voted on it. The only reason she'd voted in favor of it was because it seemed less painful than the other choices, like "Hawaiian Luau" or "Carnivale" or "Midsummer Night's Dream." But now she found that she rather liked the idea of celebrating a symbolic new year.

Thirty-nine. Thirty-eight. Thirty-seven. The scoreboard in the gymnasium ticked off the seconds. It really felt like New Year's Eve. There were hats, and noisemakers, and streamers, and confetti, and hundreds of balloons in nets hanging from the ceiling ready to be dropped at the stroke of twelve. And all the girls looked beautiful in their prom dresses, and all the guys handsome in tuxedos.

Mel could feel the excitement in the room as the seconds slipped away, as the past receded, and the future loomed full of hope and promise. There was a part of her that wished she could erase the past. But she realized that the past was the foundation for all she was and all she ever would be. And while there had been sadness, there had been much more happiness.

Phil reached over and took Mel's hand. He was her date for the evening. Not a real date, just two friends pretending to be a couple because neither one of them had a real date. But there was no one in the world with whom Mel would rather have been than Phil. She felt safe with him, and comfortable. She was grateful to have him in her life. And even though he wasn't a real date, she couldn't help feeling that he was the most handsome guy there.

"*Ten, nine, eight*," the crowd roared, shaking the room.

Phil nudged Mel and gestured with his eyes toward Stacey and Eric. They were counting as enthusiastically as everybody else. It was good to see them having fun, if only for the evening. It was going to take a long time for all of them to get over what had happened. Especially Stacey. Not only had she been hurt, and personally traumatized, she'd also lost her brother. She was going to need a lot of help, and a lot of support. And fortunately, she would be surrounded by friends who could give her that. The Pattersons made the decision not to move after all, as much for Stacey's sake as their own. They realized that it would be better for all of them to stay where they were, where they had friends and family to help them recover.

"*Three, two, one. Happy New Year*," the cry went up, as the balloons cascaded down. Mel threw her arms around Phil and kissed him. Then she did the same with Stacey. And Eric. And she and Stacey watched with amusement as Phil and Eric did that handshake-hug-pat-on-the-back thing guys do to show affection for one another. And there were exchanges of affection with other friends, too.

Then the band started in on the last song of the evening. Phil swept Mel into his arms in a playfully gallant gesture. And they began swaying in time with the music.

"May old acquaintance be forgot," the singer intoned. "And never brought to mind."

Mel couldn't help thinking about Bobby Crawford. She would never forget him. Even after the tragedy he'd caused, she couldn't hate him. She hoped that someday he would be able to make a life for himself, and forget about the one he'd lost, the life he should have led, that was so cruelly stollen from him. Mel couldn't help but pity Bobby Crawford. He should have grown up with them. He should have known the warmth, and love, and comfort that they had enjoyed all their lives. He should have had friendships that lasted a lifetime. Friendships that Mel was sure would last the rest of their lives.

"What are you thinking about?" Phil said, looking into her eyes.

"Just us." Mel smiled at him. "And how lucky we all are to have one another."

Phil smiled back at her and held her in his gaze. She knew what he was thinking, knew what he was feeling. Because she was thinking and feeling the very same things. And even before he moved, she knew what he was going to do.

He kissed her. Not the way he had before. Not like a best friend. But like a real date. And for a moment she was frightened, and confused, and she almost pulled away. But it felt too good, too right. And long overdue. So instead, she just gave in to the inevitable. After all they'd been through together, a little romance couldn't possibly hurt their relationship.

TERRIFYING TALES OF SPINE-TINGLING SUSPENSE

THE MAN WHO WAS POE Avi
71192-3/ $3.99 US/ $4.99 Can

DYING TO KNOW Jeff Hammer
76143-2/ $3.50 US/ $4.50 Can

NIGHT CRIES Barbara Steiner
76990-5/ $3.50 US/ $4.25 Can

CHAIN LETTER Christopher Pike
89968-X/ $3.99 US/ $4.99 Can

THE EXECUTIONER Jay Bennett
79160-9/ $3.99 US/ $4.99 Can

THE LAST LULLABY Jesse Osburn
77317-1/ $3.99 US/ $4.99 Can

THE DREAMSTALKER Barbara Steiner
76611-6/ $3.50 US/ $4.25 Can

Buy these books at your local bookstore or use this coupon for ordering:

Mail to: Avon Books, Dept BP, Box 767, Rte 2, Dresden, TN 38225 D
Please send me the book(s) I have checked above.
❑ My check or money order—no cash or CODs please—for $__________ is enclosed (please add $1.50 to cover postage and handling for each book ordered—Canadian residents add 7% GST).
❑ Charge my VISA/MC Acct#__________________ Exp Date______________
Minimum credit card order is two books or $7.50 (please add postage and handling charge of $1.50 per book—Canadian residents add 7% GST). For faster service, call 1-800-762-0779. Residents of Tennessee, please call 1-800-633-1607. Prices and numbers are subject to change without notice. Please allow six to eight weeks for delivery.

Name______________________________
Address____________________________
City______________ State/Zip______________
Telephone No.______________ THO 0595

SPINE-TINGLING SUSPENSE FROM AVON FLARE

NICOLE DAVIDSON

THE STALKER	76645-0/ $3.50 US/ $4.50 Can
CRASH COURSE	75964-0/ $3.99 US/ $4.99 Can
WINTERKILL	75965-9/ $3.99 US/ $4.99 Can
DEMON'S BEACH	76644-2/ $3.50 US/ $4.25 Can
FAN MAIL	76995-6/ $3.50 US/ $4.50 Can
SURPRISE PARTY	76996-4/ $3.50 US/ $4.50 Can
NIGHT TERRORS	72243-7/ $3.99 US/ $4.99 Can

THE BAND
by Carmen Adams 77328-7/ $3.99 US/ $4.99 Can

SHOW ME THE EVIDENCE
by Alane Ferguson 70962-7/ $3.99 US/ $4.99 Can

EVIL IN THE ATTIC
by Linda Piazza 77576-X/ $3.99 US/ $4.99 Can

Buy these books at your local bookstore or use this coupon for ordering:

Mail to: Avon Books, Dept BP, Box 767, Rte 2, Dresden, TN 38225 D
Please send me the book(s) I have checked above.
❑ My check or money order—no cash or CODs please—for $__________is enclosed (please add $1.50 to cover postage and handling for each book ordered—Canadian residents add 7% GST).
❑ Charge my VISA/MC Acct#__________Exp Date__________
Minimum credit card order is two books or $7.50 (please add postage and handling charge of $1.50 per book—Canadian residents add 7% GST). For faster service, call 1-800-762-0779. Residents of Tennessee, please call 1-800-633-1607. Prices and numbers are subject to change without notice. Please allow six to eight weeks for delivery.

Name__________
Address__________
City__________State/Zip__________
Telephone No.__________ YAH 0895

Other Avon Flare Books by Award-winning Author

RON KOERTGE

THE ARIZONA KID

An ALA Best Book

70776-4/$3.50 US/ $4.25 Can

THE BOY IN THE MOON

An ALA Best Book

71474-4/$3.99 US/ $4.99 Can

MARIPOSA BLUES

71761-1/$3.50 US/ $4.25 Can

WHERE THE KISSING NEVER STOPS

An ALA Best Book

71796-4/$3.99 US/$4.99 Can

THE HARMONY ARMS

72188-0/$3.99 US/$4.99 Can

Buy these books at your local bookstore or use this coupon for ordering:

Mail to: Avon Books, Dept BP, Box 767, Rte 2, Dresden, TN 38225 D

Please send me the book(s) I have checked above.

❑ My check or money order—no cash or CODs please—for $____________is enclosed (please add $1.50 to cover postage and handling for each book ordered—Canadian residents add 7% GST).

❑ Charge my VISA/MC Acct#________________________Exp Date________________

Minimum credit card order is two books or $7.50 (please add postage and handling charge of $1.50 per book—Canadian residents add 7% GST). For faster service, call 1-800-762-0779. Residents of Tennessee, please call 1-800-633-1607. Prices and numbers are subject to change without notice. Please allow six to eight weeks for delivery.

Name____

Address_______________________________________

City______________________State/Zip____________________

Telephone No.__________________ RK 0595

The Enchanting Story
Loved By Millions
Is Now A Major Motion Picture

LYNNE REID BANKS'

THE INDIAN IN THE CUPBOARD

It all started with a birthday present Omri didn't want—a small, plastic Indian that was no use to him at all. But an old wooden cupboard and a special key brought his unusual toy to life.

Read all of the fantastic adventures of Omri and *The Indian in the Cupboard*

THE INDIAN IN THE CUPBOARD
72558-4/$3.99 US/$4.99 Can

THE RETURN OF THE INDIAN
72593-2/$3.99 US

THE SECRET OF THE INDIAN
72594-0/$3.99 US

THE MYSTERY OF THE CUPBOARD
72595-9/$3.99 US/$4.99 Can

Buy these books at your local bookstore or use this coupon for ordering:

Mail to: Avon Books, Dept BP, Box 767, Rte 2, Dresden, TN 38225 D
Please send me the book(s) I have checked above.
❑ My check or money order—no cash or CODs please—for $___________is enclosed (please add $1.50 to cover postage and handling for each book ordered—Canadian residents add 7% GST).
❑ Charge my VISA/MC Acct#____________________Exp Date______________
Minimum credit card order is two books or $7.50 (please add postage and handling charge of $1.50 per book—Canadian residents add 7% GST). For faster service, call 1-800-762-0779. Residents of Tennessee, please call 1-800-633-1607. Prices and numbers are subject to change without notice. Please allow six to eight weeks for delivery.

Name______________________________
Address____________________________
City_______________State/Zip______________
Telephone No._______________ IND 0895